In the spring of 1960 an English girl, Rose Nicholson, arrives in the grey world of People's Poland. Ostensibly on holiday, she comes with important news for her elder sister, Janet Rudowska, who was married during the war to a university teacher, now a party member. The Rudowskis have a fourteen-year-old son, Tadeusz, whose entire future may depend on the results of Rose's visit.

The Ice Saints is the story of what happens to the four of them when the moral and emotional demands of Rose's England come into conflict with the old and new conventions of a people's democracy: these are represented not only by Rose's brother-in-law, but by all the other people, from young students to members of the pre-war aristocracy, with whom Rose becomes involved during her stay.

Frank Tuohy's exact eye for the English abroad and his sombre affection for the people who inhabit the paradox of contemporary Poland have already been noticed in his brilliant collection of stories *The Admiral and the Nuns*. In this, his third novel, he tells a story which is sad, funny and quietly ferocious.

THE ICE SAINTS

BY

FRANK TUOHY

CONTEMPORARY FICTION
MACMILLAN AND CO LTD
London 1966

This Contemporary Fiction edition was produced in 1966 for sale to its members only by the proprietors, Readers Union Ltd, at Aldine House, 10-13 Bedford Street, London W.C.2 and at Letchworth Garden City, Herts. Full details of membership may be obtained from our London address. The book is set in 11 point Linotype Baskerville leaded and has been reprinted by The Northumberland Press, Gateshead upon Tyne. It was first published by Macmillan and Co Ltd.

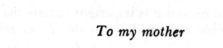

To my mother

One

THE drawing-room was entirely English. The Office of Works had provided deep armchairs, a sofa you could have slept on, though of course nobody had ever done so, and a low glass-topped table. The only exotic things lay on this table: a bowl of arctic anemones, and three or four consecutive copies of the *Times* and the *Guardian* for a week in April, 1960. These had recently been torn from their postal wrappers and were still half-unrolled.

Between chintz curtains the windows looked out hopefully, as though on to herbaceous borders planted ready for the spring. But it was like being back-stage, where the scenery comes to an end. There was an iron fence topped with barbed wire, and a wall of yellow, unpointed brickwork, which was beginning to crumble away. The street was paved with stone and opposite stood a ruin, pockmarked by gunfire from long ago. At some distance were large grey buildings and over them a greyer sky.

The sky is enormous in those parts. Its huge arch covers the city and the great river and the flat sandy plain on which pinewoods and heath and infertile fields stretch out as far as the horizon. Patches of exactly the same landscape can be seen at intervals from Aldershot and Camberley, across Belgium and Pomerania and up to the Russian frontier. It is military country, beloved by the organizers of manœuvres and battles. Its dry gullies are as convenient for

1   A*

firing squads as for lovers; its bracken and heather are more accustomed to mortar fire than to the minor conflagrations caused by picnickers, and its deadly fauna include the adder and the unexploded grenade.

Pine logs from these forests were crackling in the drawing room fireplace and a young woman was standing in front of it, talking.

This young woman stood on the outsides of her feet with her hands clasped behind her, as though she were still obeying a forgotten governess's injunction to straighten her shoulders. She was ungainly, badly dressed and her voice was shrill and discordant, but she had a perfect skin and a rather beautiful face. She could only have been what she was, a confident member of the British ruling class.

' Thank God you've come both of you, I must say. Because I'm here all alone until Mark comes back. He'll be late because of this girl, this friend of his sister's we're looking after. Do please sit down, Miss Er — Mark's gone to the airport to pick her up. Does that sound nasty, Adam? You speak English so much better than we all do. Does that sound nasty when I say Mark's gone to the airport to pick her up? '

' Alexandra, it sounds wonderful when you are saying it.'

' Hum! '

She had asked for the clumsy compliment, yet seemed bored by it.

The man who had spoken was over middle size; he had black curly hair, a square face, with a nose which curved up like a saddle. When he smiled he showed a steel tooth, and sometimes his pale eyes gave the false impression that he wore contact lenses.

' Look, do come nearer the fire, Miss Er — '

' Handisyde.'

'What are you going to drink?'

'I'd just love a real Polish Vodka.'

'Adam will have a dry martini because he always does. Adam, give Miss Handisyde a real Polish Vodka, will you?' Alexandra returned to her stance in front of the hearth. 'How have you been getting on, I'm sure Adam has been filling your ears with all sorts of subversion.'

The guest, having got through a smoker's cough, bowed her short-cut, greying head as though she were beginning to recite: 'Well, this has really been a most wonderful experience. I don't think I've ever met people who seem so'— she gestured with rough hands—'I can't express how much'—

Alexandra looked down at her cheerfully. 'I know. I'm just like that. But I'm sure you'll find it's quite all right the moment you get back home. Look at me. When I'm here I can hardly think of anything to say at all, but the moment we got to London at Christmas the whole thing became absolutely and completely clear to me. I mean, I simply felt I was a one-girl bureau, don't you know, of Iron Curtain affairs. Of course I do speak the language much better than Mark does, and that does help.'

'For instance, we spent some time this morning with a really interesting man. I'm afraid I don't quite remember his name. Adam darling, what was that man's name again?'

Adam Karpinski was standing between the women, watching them with attention and wonder, as if they had been two fireworks, two set-pieces, which he had managed to set off in conjunction. Neither, he thought as his gaze moved from one to the other, could have fulfilled the exotic roles he had given them with more perfect timing and intonation. Only his glee at this must be always unshared, because there were few people around who spoke and appreciated English as well as he did.

'Which man do you mean, Margaret?'

'The man at that place we went to this morning. With those column things. They weren't columns really,' she said to Alexandra.

'I'm sure they weren't.'

'What was that place called, Adam?'

'Which place, Margaret?'

'Oh, it doesn't matter really. But it was fascinating, I was most impressed. I intend in my report to emphasize most, most— You can't believe it, when you think.'

'Oh, I can.'

A car drew up in the street outside.

'That must be Mark. I wonder if he found Rose. Rose is this girl. Please be nice to her, Adam. There was something quite interesting I wanted to tell you about her, only unfortunately there hasn't been time.'

'I'll be very nice to her, Alexandra.'

'Of course she may be awful.' Alexandra was silent and a lost, crazy look came over her face as though stumbling, hurrying on, she had reached a part of the forest she had never expected to see. 'I've never met her. Of course, she may be quite awful.'

Mark Tatham came in, a little disarranged, pushing a handkerchief up his sleeve.

'Washing her hands. Plane was late.'

He immediately went over to Miss Handisyde, and began the effort of engaging her in conversation.

Bringing him a drink, Alexandra interrupted: 'Does she want to stay the night? Because if so, Simon has been sleeping in the spare bedroom and I'll have to tell Nanny.'

When Tatham looked up, his long white face was lined

with strain and tiredness. ' No. She's going to Biala Gora on this evening's plane. Apparently they are expecting her.'

' Poor girl, I must say. Why is she going to Biala Gora? '

' Don't speak against that place, Alexandra. I may be deserting you all to go there one day soon.'

' Oh, Adam, no. What will we all do without you? '

Alexandra stood in her old place on the hearthrug but now with her legs crossed and the outsides of her feet laid together. Her colour was high, her eyes bright and fearsome.

' Have I been there, Adam? ' Miss Handisyde asked.

' No, Margaret.'

' I seem to have been just about everywhere. As I say it's been the most fascinating — I must say the spirit of the people, that's what I find amazing. I'm going to put all that in my report when I get back. They may have political problems but they've got spirit.' She stared at her empty glass. ' That sounds rather funny, doesn't it? '

Alexandra snatched the glass from her. Karpinski followed across the room.

' My dear, it's simply all the time,' he whispered. ' We buy only the best Wodka Wyborowa, with real pounds and dollars, at the Grand Hotel kiosk every morning. And furthermore she keeps wanting to s-l-e-e-p with me.'

This joke about the spelling out of simple words he had been amused to adopt from Alexandra herself: she had inherited it from a nurseryful of sisters, the daughters of a pre-war Conservative minister.

' Adam, no! How ghastly.'

' What was it you were going to tell me about this girl? '

' It's just that — ' she broke off. ' Here she is.'

Two

'MISS HANDISYDE, this is Rose Nicholson. Mr. Karpinski. This is Elizabeth's friend. Darling, do give Rose something to drink. Rose, are you quite certain you can't stay, I mean it's so simply, really, Simon can have Nanny's bedroom, Nanny'll be quite glad to go into the night nursery and we can move Juliet's cot out into the —'

Alexandra tried to present this girl, who was extremely pretty, as just somebody else that she and Mark were obliged to deal with. The girl, however, seemed unwilling to be managed.

'No. I have already booked my place on the aeroplane.'

Alexandra's voice trailed irritably away. There was a small silence while they all watched Rose. The world outside was still with her. How long, they were thinking, would she keep that slightly abstracted look of self-assurance? Miss Handisyde was quite forgotten. Adam Karpinski moved slowly across the room towards Rose.

'Alexandra tells me that you are travelling to Biala Gora.'

'Yes. My sister is married to someone at the University there.'

Karpinski looked puzzled. 'I have heard that there is an Englishman. But I did not think he was a married man.'

'But he's a Pole. My brother-in-law, is, I mean.'

Karpinski emitted the three humming notes by which his

countrymen express dubiety and surprise. 'I see. And she has been there a long time?'

'Ten years. No, twelve. Janet is older than me.'

'Obviously, if I may say so. I wonder, is she happy there?'

'Well, perhaps not at first. But everything is much better now, isn't it?'

'Some people try to think so.'

Rose dismissed any attempt to discourage her. 'I'm looking forward to getting to Biala Gora.'

Alexandra came up and said something like 'Biawa'. 'Did I do it right, Adam?'

'Alexandra's dark "l"s are always very nicely formed.'

Alexandra took Rose's arm and led her into the dining-room.

'Rose, how I wish I was you. She's going off to the real world where we've never even been. We just see all the same people at all the parties here. Rose, I wish I was you, I do really.'

Karpinski said: 'And do you imagine that you could see how people in fact live? The moment you go to their flats they would bring out the food they have bought on the Black Market and the Nescafé from the Komis shop and they are wearing the clothes their cousin sends them from America.'

'Adam, you are so depressing. Why does Adam always have to be so depressing?'

During luncheon Rose was so placed that she could not help watching the short-haired elderly Englishwoman opposite her. After a few more incoherences, Miss Handisyde gave up all attempts at conversation; her head bowed, her hand fell dead-heavy on the table, upsetting her empty glass which rolled on to its side.

The newcomer had no idea of the importance of all this to any of the others but soon she noticed signs of a jubilant conspiracy between Adam Karpinski and Alexandra, who was blinking and shaking with almost imperceptible giggles.

She turned to Mark. His sister Elizabeth was one of her best friends but she had not seen him since his marriage; there was an altered stateliness about his bearing, as though one might hope for kindness but not humour from him. Now Mark winked at her gently and after a little he too began to tremble with laughter. The rest of the meal went as a sort of wild burlesque in which every conventional remark bubbled with hysteria. Adam Karpinski kept nudging Rose and mopping his eyes.

Finally Alexandra helped Miss Handisyde out of the room, and after a moment Karpinski followed them.

Still laughing, Mark said: 'I'm awfully sorry about all this, Rose.'

'Who on earth is she?'

'I don't know. A progressive journalist. One of these people who get wished on to one.'

'Is she always like this, I wonder.'

'Perhaps not. Odd things happen to people when they arrive here. Either they hole up in the Grand or the Bristol, complaining of tummy-aches and demanding to see the Embassy doctor — who isn't, of course, allowed to see them. Or they find that vodka is the best way out.'

'But why?'

'Shock.'

'I haven't felt any. Ought I to?'

'Delayed. No, honestly I expect you've got enough to occupy your mind as it is.'

The girl looked relieved that the conversation had at length turned to the only thing she could talk about.

'Yes. I still don't know what I'm going to do. There's one or two things I must be sure of.'

'We'll do our best to help. The Embassy lawyer—' He stopped, seeing that Karpinski had returned to the room.

'Mark, I really do apologize most profoundly. I've seen this crisis approaching but the old girl was simply insisting on coming to luncheon here. Keeping in with the jolly old Embassy, you know. It is too very bad that it should happen in your house. Alexandra has most kindly offered to drive us back to the Grand Hotel.'

He picked up his wine glass and drained it off.

'Still, if she passes right out, it at least means I may have a rest this afternoon. And tomorrow morning, thank God, she is off to Prague.' He turned to Rose. 'I was thinking, is your brother-in-law perhaps called Witold Rudowski?'

'Yes, he is.'

'I see. Then perhaps we shall meet again. I am frequently in Biala Gora.'

'Oh good.' She sounded pleased. She liked him. With his vivid smiles and his air of tightly-packed energy, he was quite unlike the glum exiles one saw in South Kensington.

'That's rather strange, isn't it?' Rose asked Mark when the other had gone.

'Everybody knows everybody else in this country. The trouble starts when they don't know what everybody else is up to. Let's have some coffee.'

While Mark fetched a bottle of brandy and a couple of glasses Rose sat staring unhappily in front of her.

'Cheer up. Have some brandy.'

'Thank you. All the same I do hope I'm not going to get drunk or have tummy-aches.'

'Well, if you do, you need only come running back here. Alexandra would love to have you.'

There was a moment's pause between them, sufficiently protracted to throw some doubt on this.

'Thank you,' Rose said again. 'You see the trouble is I'm so frightened of breaking this news to Janet.'

'How long since you've seen her?'

'Two years. Of course none of this was in the air then. Aunt Louise was still alive, though we'd none of us set eyes on her for ages.' Rose cautiously sipped at her brandy. 'Janet came home when my father was dying and we were pretty much taken up with that.'

'Your sister doesn't know anything about it, then?'

'No. She thinks I'm just here for fun. She always spoke about not mentioning important things in letters. This *is* an important thing, isn't it? Somehow, now I'm actually here, it doesn't seem so terribly important after all.'

'You were quite right not to mention it. *They* would think it terribly important.'

'Why?'

'That's what we must ask the lawyer ultimately. Roughly something like this: legally any property, monies (I wonder why one always says monies) etcetera owned by a national abroad must be realized and transferred into local currency. I don't know which exchange rate it'd be at, but there wouldn't be much left.'

'I'm sure we don't want to do that.'

'Then you have to be careful who you talk to. You're breaking the law. Someone may object.'

'Who?'

'What about your sister's husband?'

He spoke with a hint of distaste. The Poles these English

women married were always reprehensible, and to be admitted to the discussion as late as possible.

'Witek? Why should he object? I don't know. He came back here after the war when all his friends stayed in England, so we were always frightfully suspicious. And then they sent such cheerful letters, during the Stalin period. I liked him as far as I can remember. I was only a child.'

'He's doubtful, then?'

'I suppose so. Of course he may have changed.'

'You can't tell about people here. They'll protest any amount of pro-Western feeling but you can't expect them to do anything about it. Why should they? Their best hope is to go on with things as they are.'

Rose thought for a moment and said: 'Well, that simply doesn't apply to the Rudowski family any more. Everything is altered. Decisions have to be made. I suppose it's Janet who must make them.'

'Is she expecting this?'

'No, not at all. You see, my great-aunt thought women with money were a prey to fortune-hunters. She was only going to leave her money to men. We knew she meant to leave something to Nicholas. He was my brother. He was killed in the war.'

'So you're the herald angel?'

'I suppose so. I feel scared of the whole thing. The solicitors insisted I should come.'

'There wasn't any other way, Rose. You couldn't write letters. I'm sure you'll find the best solution in the end.'

'It's strange, with a thing like this. You feel grim but happy. Think, after all the Rudowskis have been through, to be saved by a bit of money.'

'How much?'

'The solicitors think it'll be almost fifteen thousand.'

'You don't know for certain?'

'Probate hasn't been given yet. But it'll be a lot to them. It would be to me.'

Mark smiled, hesitated and said: 'Rose, you possibly may find they don't consider it as important as you do. After all, money means such different things in different places.'

Rose remembered that Alexandra was very rich.

'Of course if it were changed into local currency its value would be only a third. £5,000 can't be a lot, even here.'

'You'll have to see.' He stood up. 'Be careful who you tell, that's all. There's Alexandra back. We'd better leave for the airport quite soon.'

Alexandra came in, pulling off a round fur hat.

'We got her up in the lift and I left her being very sick. Adam spoke to the chambermaid and to the old horror in the navy sateen dress who sits at the end of each corridor and spies on you. She must have got a lot on old Handisyde, if all Adam says is true. Oh Rose, poor you, do sit down and tell us all about Elizabeth. How is she? You've been swigging brandy. Without me. Let me get a glass.'

'Rose and I must go to the airport almost at once.'

'Must you?'

'We've been talking about Rose's trip.'

'Have you, it's really too exciting, isn't it?'

'All the same, darling, I don't think anyone else should know about it, except us.'

Alexandra picked a dead flower out of the bowl of blue anemones. 'No, of course not. Though I can't imagine who'd be interested, can you?'

'They might.' Mark looked at his watch. 'Will you be needing the car, darling? Because I'll take Rose to the airport and then go back to the office. If you want it, come with us.'

Alexandra went on pulling out shrivelled flowers. 'The children and Nanny picked these, but they don't last. What's that? No, I don't need the car. Goodbye, Rose.'

Three

OUT of the small window with its doll's house curtains,
Rose noticed several hares loping away into the spring
grass; they looked very large in the evening light, their
shadows stretching out towards the runway. Then the aeroplane humped and jolted to a halt. The passengers, who included three priests in raincoats and cloth caps, at once
stood up and began pushing towards the door. The smell of
winter clothes and tobacco and people, the whole very
tough smell of Eastern Europe, blotted out the inward
rush of the evening air. However, when Rose stood for a
moment at the top of the iron steps, she thought she could
hear blackbirds singing.

The bus was already waiting. But first an assortment of
objects had to be hauled out of the aeroplane and resettled
beside the driver's seat: the usual newspapers and postbags;
a keg of acid; a bale of fox skins; bundles of skis; a child's
tricycle. When everything was ready they drove off through
the ploughed fields towards Biala Gora.

On the pre-1914 maps it is called Weissberg. With some
effort you could distinguish a nineteenth-century German
city among the factories which were now pumping bland
columns of smoke into the sky. You could see, among the
new blocks of flats, large houses divided into tenements and
falling into ruin; they stood in gardens where the trees had
been damaged by shell-fire and the earth had long ago been

14

stamped naked and hard. The old market-place, where the airport bus stopped, had been blown up by the retreating armies; now, under a maze of scaffolding, it was being restored.

Rose and Tadeusz recognized each other immediately, for photographs had been exchanged at intervals. He was fifteen, with reddish hair and a narrow white face. He kissed her confidently on both cheeks.

' Hadn't we better take a taxi? '

' It is not necessary. I may carry your luggage.'

' I'm afraid it's very heavy.'

' That is nothing.' He gathered breath and said in a rush: ' Only last week, for instance, I was skiing in Tatry mountains. We made thirty-one kilometres with packs on our backs. We saw a bear.'

' How exciting.'

' Yes, it was very interesting. Most of the bears live now in Czechoslovakia. Mostly they are coming here only in summertime.'

Rose's suitcases were put on the pavement. They were clean and expensive among the others of bursting cardboard. The boy picked them both up. She could see it was an effort for him but knew it would be no good asking him to give in.

' I expect they come for their holidays, like me.'

' Please? '

' The bears.'

The boy frowned, and before she could explain he had started off through the crowd, as though pulled forward by the momentum of the two swinging cases. Rose followed as best she could. Her shoes, though they had low tapered heels, were not good on the broken pavements. She was wearing a heavy-knit sweater and, since it was a mild evening, she soon began to feel hot, and uneasy at the stares of the people who passed them. She was shocked, too, at their difference from herself. Most were dressed in little more than rags, jumble-sale clothes. There was no effort, such as you might find in a southern country, to present a façade of prosperity to the world. Each seemed to show a face and figure which said: 'Look, this is me, smashed.' And her nephew, with his fierce unhealthy look, fitted easily into this background.

Once he stopped for a moment and jerked his head, without letting go of her cases. 'Over there is the Popular Comedy Theatre. They are playing "A Policeman Calls" by J. B. Priestley.'

'You mean "An Inspector Calls".'

'Perhaps.'

He scowled and began walking again. After this, she was careful not to correct him about his knowledge of English things.

Near the market-place there had been two or three massive State department stores, and an occasional scribble of neon lighting. Now the city grew darker and dingier. Small shops crouched half-hidden under greyish-black buildings. The buildings which had stucco on them appeared to have been kicked systematically round the base of the walls, where they showed a surface of crumbling brick. Others were built only of brick, cracked and diminished by the weather.

'Look, please let's take a taxi. I've been travelling all day.'

'If you like we may take the tram.'

Thinking that Tadeusz was still worrying about Priestley's play, she dared not object. But even the tram ride seemed to take longer than was conceivable. Everybody stared at Rose, who stood with her eyes downcast. She felt

impossibly far from England, and even from the Tathams'
house in the capital. Only to imagine Alexandra here would
be absurd, and all Mark's considered advice seemed to refer
to nothing at all. Rose's elation at her arrival had gone.
Instead she quaked with nerves at the prospect of meeting
her sister.

Janet, who was twelve years older than Rose, had trained
as a nurse and met Witek in a war hospital. Their son
Tadeusz was born in England but the Rudowskis had
proudly bestowed on him a name that could not be
anglicized. Janet, like many nurses, had always been un-
questioningly kind to everyone, and her kindness had led
her to this war-pocked city in Eastern Europe.

At thirty-six Janet had the thickened body of a woman in
late middle age. She clung to Rose with hands that were
like claws. Emotion welled up, originating from the separa-
tion, but due as much, in Rose's case, to physical exhaustion.

Very soon after, however, the staff nurse's briskness came
out once more and Rose recognized it with affection. ' Witek
has the front room all to himself now. His books are there,
of course. You and I'll sleep in here.'

The room they were standing in had divans along two of
the walls. There was a round table in the middle of the
room, some potted plants, dog-eared American magazines;
a shelf of Janet's favourite books from her childhood, and
copies of Eckersley's *Brighter English*, Allen's *Living English Structure* and Jespersen's *Growth and Structure of the
English Language*. The furniture had a poverty-engrained
look like the furniture in very cheap lodgings.

' This is where I work, really, so you'll have to move out
during the day. But I'm sure Witek won't mind you sitting
in his room while he's at the University.'

'Where does Tadeusz go?'

'He's on a camp bed in the kitchen. He's fine there, frightfully tidy. He gets it from me. Well, now you know how we stand. There are some hangers for your clothes in the hallway. And I've cleared you out a couple of drawers. I packed the things into an old trunk, actually. Do you know, I've still got my school trunk, the one I had at Cheltenham. I don't know why I keep it really. It isn't as though I was ever likely to move anywhere any more. Is that all right, then?'

'I'm sorry, darling, I simply must go somewhere.'

'Oh dear, I've got out of the habit of asking. They never ask you here. The aunt is through the kitchen.'

The place was not clean, and squares of newspaper were pushed on to a nail. The printed language looked frightening, so utterly unknown.

Janet took such pride in her arrangements that you had to accept them without question. Rose remembered Mark Tatham's warnings about drink. I'll need about half a bottle, she thought, before I dare tell her that from now on, all this can come to an end.

The moment he had delivered Rose to the flat, Tadeusz stepped backwards and disappeared into the dusk. He and Witek were both absent for supper. Rose thought this was insufferably rude and it was almost too much for her waning self-confidence. While they drank tea and ate cold ham with very good bread and butter, Janet talked on.

'Do they all do their eyes like this now?'

'Like what?'

'You know — mascara. I saw it in those *Vogues* you send me but I thought it was only for models. I mean, I wasn't to know, living here, was I?' She seemed on the defensive as though everything that had happened was her own fault.

Rose noticed that Janet still held her knife like a fountain pen, the way nurses did, and remembered how her father used to tease her about it. Watching her while they ate, she was all at once overwhelmed by pity for Janet. She needed the attentions of their childhood, hot milk and biscuits, an early night. Could you get biscuits here or even milk? From Janet's conversation she gathered that the extent of one's deprivations was so enormous as to be only a subject for jokes. You could only suggest something for her to deny its possibility with a hard laugh. Rose was sure that this bitterness was something new, that it had not been there when Janet last came to England.

'I have to pay twenty zlotys duty on each of them.'

'On what?'

'The *Vogues*. But it's worth it. You see I give them to my dressmaker. She copies the patterns and she alters things or makes them up for me free, from time to time. You've got to be smart about things like that in this place, I can tell you.' She poured out more tea. 'Not much supper tonight, I'm afraid. You see I had my evening lessons earlier, to be free when you came. No time for shopping.'

'The ham was jolly good.'

Rose was miserable. Her father and she had comforted themselves for some years with the idea that Janet's stoical cheeriness made her life here somehow possible. Evidently this was not so. Rose tried to cheer herself by thinking that her own arrival had made Janet homesick — she had always surrendered easily to the simpler emotions — and this had turned her against her surroundings. Whatever was to happen to the Rudowskis now, Janet was too emotional to be permitted to have her own way. She had to be told, but it was Witek and of course Tadeusz who were the ones to decide.

Four

WHEN Witold Rudowski finally returned from England in 1948, it was proposed that he would head the new Department of English Philology at Biala Gora University. But the plan came to nothing. Next year two departments of English at other universities were closed and their staffs dismissed. Except in the capital, all teaching of English above the elementary level ceased. Witek instead received the post of arranging and conducting translation classes for the other departments at Biala Gora. His colleagues were mostly elderly ladies in destitution, who had once had English governesses or had been to convents in England. He found himself guiding young historians in translating from English translations of Marx and Lenin or from original texts by Howard Fast and Jack Lindsay.

During these years Janet and he lived by teaching privately and by doing translations for official publications. When more English was permitted in the secondary schools he quickly wrote a text book which was accepted by the Ministry of Education. It was not a very satisfactory book and he realized its imperfections sooner than anyone. But this led him to a more detailed study of phonetics and intonation and idiomatic expressions. He was a man who, once he took something up, became easily obsessed by it and devoted himself to it to the exclusion of everything else. In spite of having a foreign wife, Rudowski survived the difficult years without danger, and although exhausted from overwork he conducted his course at the University with an efficiency which shone beside the amateurish efforts of his colleagues. He went to the political meetings and seminars which were numerous at that time, feeling that he ought to be interested, and survived them in a state of torpid inattention like a public schoolboy in Chapel. As with so many hardworking people, he did not have quite enough time to bother about what was happening to his colleagues who failed to adapt to the régime.

When after 1956 a new proposal was made for a Chair of English at Biala Gora, Witek was the obvious choice of candidate. He alone had continued with English studies all the time. He was supported at the University by several influential people, including Dr. Zwiersz, the representative of the Party. And he had good friends in the Ministry of Higher Education whom he was always visiting with plans for student exchanges or for holiday courses to be directed by himself, which they politely pigeonholed.

Against him, however, was a faction which included Professor Markiewicz, the international lawyer and present Rector of the University, old Professor Barcik, of the Chair of Comparative Philology, and their supporters. Rudowski had done nothing which they considered to be a work of serious scholarship. His doctoral thesis, which he had put together hurriedly after his return to his native land, was an ill-constructed effort entitled 'H. G. Wells: Prophet of Revolution'. It had been accepted at Warsaw University but the Professors here did not think much of Warsaw. Above all — this, though not consciously formulated by any of them, was always at the back of their minds — Rudowski had nothing of the *mana* which surrounds a professor.

In a society which now considered itself to be classless but which still paid respect to its intellectuals, this aspect of university life had increased in importance with the years. One elderly man might be surrounded by half a dozen assistants, former pupils, usually women, who typed his manuscripts, brought him mushrooms from the country and tried to keep on good terms with his wife. His influence would also be felt among his male disciples not only in Poland but in the Polish diaspora at universities in North and South America. How could you imagine Rudowski in a position like this? Choosing him for the Chair would in fact diminish themselves, the professors thought.

Witold Rudowski was short and square, and his hair and skin had the same pale almost colourless look. A true Silesian, he came from the border country near Biala Gora where there had always been a strong German influence. But traditional characteristics must have been dormant in him, because already Tadeusz looked like a nineteenth century patriot on the barricades.

Witek kissed Rose affectionately and asked her about her journey.

'Tadeusz met you all right? He always gets everything wrong.'

'Oh perfectly. And I recognized him at once.'

'Would we have recognized you, I wonder. Your photo-graph does not do justice to you.'

'I photograph terribly badly.'

'I thought that last one was very good,' Janet said.

'You must excuse my not being present when you arrived. You see, I had a meeting of the lecturers at the University. In any case I thought the two sisters would like to have the evening to themselves.'

'But I expect we'll have lots of time together.'

'Darling, I must tell you I've got lessons nearly all tomorrow. Zosia cooks lunch for us at about two.'

'I'll be all right. Please, you mustn't worry about me.'

'Tomorrow, let me show you the buildings of our university. They are not very beautiful, in a bad German style, I think.'

'I don't know if Rose is interested.'

'Oh, I am. I'd love to see them really. Not just the buildings, but to know about it all.'

'Would you like me to make some more tea, darling?'

'Perhaps Rose would prefer something stronger. I have some *jarzembiak*, a sort of vodka made with some berries. I don't know what the berry is called in English, if indeed it has an equivalent. A dictionary I have consulted on this point suggests "spindleberry" but I believe that is not probable.'

'Whatever it is, I'd love to taste it.'

While Witek went into his own room to fetch the bottle, Janet sat silent and looked offended. Rose had agreed to the last two things suggested by Witek. Was she going to have to accept each of their suggestions alternately, regardless of what she herself wanted, in order to avoid coming down on one side or the other?

Witek poured little glasses full of red liquid, for her and for himself.

'Cheerio.'

The liqueur, after a delicate summer taste, was a slow-spreading warmth.

Witek fixed Rose with a bright interested look.

'You must know that we are very anxious to know of all aspects of English life. Could you not tell us something of your experiences? Anything.' He laughed. 'The first thing that comes into your head.'

He created an atmosphere of sadness and embarrassment. The girl was determined not to wince but to help him as far as she could: Janet must really learn not to be beastly to him in front of her.

'Witek, you make things much too difficult. What is it you want to know?'

'Everything! Your work, for instance. We know so little of modern English life.'

'But you meet other English people, don't you?'

'Rarely in Biala Gora. There is Mr. Loasby, a young English scholar, who was once at our house. And when I am in Warsaw I go to see Mr. Pilkington, at the British Council, usually to borrow films and tape recordings. But Mr. Pilkington is a very busy man and has not time for many callers.'

'Oh, I thought English people came here quite often.'

'Ah ha!'

All at once he was prancing up and down in front of her, rubbing his hands together. She watched with astonishment, wondering what had happened.

'She says off-ten. She says off-ten. You see, Janet, you and Daniel Jones's dictionary are not always to be relied on.'

Janet was roused by this. 'But Rose, we all said " orphan " when we were little. Surely you did, too. Can't you remember?'

Rose, who had not appreciated why all the fuss was being made, said: 'I must have picked it up somewhere.'

'Can it be that there has been a change of usage in recent years, since, for instance, we left England? That might bear some looking into. Well, we cannot worry Rose about this. It is our profession and not hers. But what about Rose's profession? What job have you been doing, Rose?'

' Well, after Daddy died you know I went to live with this friend of mine who was at school with me, Elizabeth Tatham. I got a job as a secretary, as I'd already done typing and shorthand. But it was terribly boring. I mean there was no one you could talk to, I mean no one you could really talk to. So I gave that up and got a job with this friend of Elizabeth's. She has a sort of furniture shop and does interior decoration, that sort of thing.'

Rose felt foolish reciting all this to Witek Rudowski, on a spring evening in Biala Gora. Beauchamp Place, Knightsbridge, was at the very opposite end of the world. Witek could not possibly picture anything she was talking about and watching him she could almost see his mind still working away at the problem of ' off-ten ' and ' orphan '. She hurried through as fast as she could, chattering merely to convince Janet that she took no sides.

' Well, this friend, my friend's friend I mean, was frightfully nice but she was always going on at me. I mean I tried to stop her but in the end I had to leave. So that was one job.'

Rose laughed a little triumphantly at reaching this conclusion. Witek stood up and poured her another tot of *jarzembiak*.

' What do you mean? Was she unjust to you? Did she restrain your wages? '

' Oh no. Actually, it turned out she was a Lesbian.'

' And what is that? '

Rose was vanquished.

Janet explained briskly.

' I see.' He was genuinely shocked. He gulped and said in a strained voice: ' Thank you. I had always been meaning to look that word up.' Then, more confidently: ' I did not know that that kind of thing still went on.'

B

Rose felt a sudden wave of fondness for him.

Later, when they were in bed Janet said: 'I wish you hadn't told him you would go to the university tomorrow morning. He'll keep you there for hours, and I'd promised you'd have coffee with my friends.'

'*I've* promised now.'

'Try and get away as soon as you can.'

'Perhaps I won't want to.' Rose tried to find a comfortable position on the divan, which was hard and lumpy. 'Don't think I'm being beastly. I want to find out about things for myself.'

'I'm sorry I'm sure. I thought you came here to see me.'

Rose put her face on her elbow and looked across at the other bed. Janet was staring at the ceiling. They waited for the silence between them to turn into sleep.

Five

THE next morning Rose was hurried out at half past eight when her sister's first pupil arrived. She found Tadeusz in the kitchen, and hugged him. Afterwards, she was surprised she had done this: the previous evening she had felt he disapproved of her.

'There is tea. Mummy said, will you make eggs if you want them.'

'I don't think I do. Did you sleep well?'

'Yes. I can sleep anywhere. In February when Papa and I went to ski, we slept on the floor of a hut with twenty-six other persons. Twenty-eight of us and the stove. That was all in the hut. We carried out food on our backs.'

'Where was this? At Zakopane?'

'Everybody goes to Zakopane. This was right up in the mountains.'

'Where you saw the bear?'

'No, that was last week, in a different part of Tatry.'

'You seem to spend a lot of time on holidays.'

'Polish people like excursions. They all live too close together so when they can get away, they go. Also there are cheap tickets for students. But now I must not go so much because I am working for *matura* examination. It is very difficult, there are many subjects and I cannot do Russian. Our Russian teacher is no good, she is an old woman who was born in Kiev and looks like a pig. Nobody likes her.'

'Because she is Russian or because she looks like a pig?'

'Both. Only she is not Russian really, but Ukrainian. We do not like Ukrainians, too.'

'Either,' Rose corrected him.

'Please?'

'Either, when there are two things. You meant to say "We do not like Russians and we do not like Ukrainians either." So there are two lots you don't like.'

Tadeusz said: 'More than two. We do not like Czechs, too. And Lithuanians. And Germans. And Jews. Couldn't I say "too"?'

Rose was silenced.

He devoured a large slice of black bread smeared with very pale butter. 'If I pass *matura* examination, I will try to go to the university. Either here or in Warsaw.'

'Are you going to do English?'

'No.' He filled his glass up with tea. 'There is no English department yet at our university. Probably they will begin one soon, with Papa to teach. But what is the use of studying English if we cannot go to England?'

'I suppose not.' She looked away from him, her eyes hot with nervous excitement, and down into her glass of tea. 'What *do* you want to do, Tadeusz?'

'Engineering. Engineers can go everywhere. There is here an engineer who Mummy teaches, who was to China and India and last year he was to Ghana. He builds dams.'

'You'd like that?'

'Only for a time. I would not want to live with niggers. I always want to come back to Poland.'

Tadeusz stood up and washed his plate and glass. He came and stood beside Rose. Wherever he was, his physical presence was turned on to her, like a beam of light. He was hungry-looking. Not perhaps in the immediate physical

sense, though he was certainly thin, but because the un-
finishedness of adolescence seemed more acute in his case.
He was gasping for more of life, as though the atmosphere
he breathed lacked some chemical constituent he could
barely live any longer without.

Because of his incompleteness, he was always worried
about other people.

'How do you think Mummy is looking?'

'She seems quite well, but I think she works too hard.'

'Everyone works too hard. I think she is unhappy. Did
she love Grandfather very much?'

Rose was surprised at this. 'Yes, at least, I suppose she
loved Daddy. But not specially, if you see what I mean. You
see, she was so seldom there. Always at boarding school, or
being a nurse. I can't remember her before that.'

The boy frowned and sat down again opposite her.

'Then why has she changed so much since she was in
England two years ago?'

'Has she?'

'Do you know, all through the Stalinist time, when they
tried to collectivize the farms and there were only potatoes
to eat, and we had U.B. — that is Secret Police — watching
our house, all that time Mummy was wonderful. She hardly
ate. She put a little on her plate and went out to the kitchen
to look for something, and when she came back we had
nearly finished and she finished too. Papa did not notice,
he does not notice things like that, but I notice. You know
eight years ago I was going to have a brother but he
died because Mummy was working all the time and so
weak?'

'Yes, I knew that. Of course I didn't really know until
I came here. It is difficult to imagine these things from
outside.'

' And now everyone here is getting happier and she is still unhappy.'

' But why, Tadeusz? '

' I think it was because she went to London. It is a very beautiful place? '

' Not really.'

' I know I have been there, when I was three. To the zoo. But I can't remember.'

' Would you like to go again? '

' For a visit. But not before my exams.' He stopped, hot-faced. ' I am sorry. I talk too much. But it is not like you being my aunt.'

' I should hope not. Do you smoke? '

' Not yet.' He walked up and down the kitchen, preparing to say something. ' Since Mummy comes back from England, she does not like being Polish any more. I am very proud of being Polish. Do you know Polish history? '

' Not much, I'm afraid.'

' Later on I will tell you. What time is it? '

' Half past nine.'

' I am to take you to the University for Papa to show you round.'

' Good! Is it far away? '

' Only one kilometre. Less than last night.'

The Rudowskis' flat was on the ground floor of a block forming part of a recent housing development. Other blocks, all exactly the same, blotted out the distances, and the only way you could tell which was which was by a number roughly whitewashed beside the door. Between the blocks there was raw earth and rubble, with cinderpaths leading to an unpaved road.

It was a sunny morning and swarms of small children

were playing outside. They were still wrapped up in heavy clothes, some so solidly that their arms and legs were forced to the corners, as though they had recently been blown up with bicycle pumps. They had no toys but were apparently able to cover empty space with self-contained and purposeful activity. Further on, there was one tricycle, whose owner was riding savagely round in wide circles, isolated already in the loneliness that great possessions bring.

These children looked healthy, far healthier than Tadeusz, whom the bright sky seemed to oppress.

'We were lucky to get a new flat,' he said. 'We had to wait many years on a list.'

Rose had not realized the flat was new. Its plaster was cracked and it had already taken on the drab unpainted look of the city.

They set off away from the road, between broken-down palings and the backs of single cottages. The black earth was mostly bare but there were clumps of yellow coltsfoot. Away from the blocks of tenements, the sky looked enormous and the view to the horizon was interrupted only by the little hill that gives Biala Gora its name in German and Polish.

Rose and Tadeusz arrived at the broad Jan Kochanowski Avenue which almost encircles the town. There were market carts, some lorries and one or two taxis. The University buildings stood opposite and over the main portico was written 'Universytet Biala Gora im. J. Kochanowskiego'.

On the steps, they were stopped by a most extraordinary female. She was all of six feet tall, with a slight stoop, and dressed in a mustard-coloured knitted suit. She had bright, inquisitive eyes and a nose which gave her the look of a fierce lady-eagle.

'Tadeusz! Tadeusz? And Rose! I must call you Rose, I think, because I am already knowing you so well. How pleased our dear Janet must be, isn't Mummy pleased, Tadeusz? How lovely you are, my dear, you cannot know how exciting it is for all of us to have you here. You come to us for coffee this morning—'

'Yes, but—'

'I know, I know, dear Janet has telephoned to me already. What must be, must be. But it is all right, we are doing it then instead this afternoon. Tadeusz will bring you—'

Tadeusz looked uncomfortable. They had not yet enough confidence in each other to unite against this stranger.

'No,' Rose said quickly. 'Give me the address and I'll find it.'

The café turned out to be in the market-square.

'I'll be there,' Rose said. If she did not go, Janet would be angry with her. It was obvious that promises had been made for her, expectations were to be fulfilled.

'My dear, that is wonderful. Only a few of us. Janet's true friends. We are all so excited and we hope you will be so happy here. How long do you stay?'

'My visa's for two months.'

When she had gone, Rose said: 'People think I'm a fool, incapable of moving round by myself.'

'I must study with my colleagues this afternoon.'

'I know. I feel guilty about keeping you from work. Who is that woman, anyway?'

'She is Mrs. Kazimierska. Her husband is a doctor here. She is Mummy's greatest friend.'

'You don't like her much?'

'She talks very much. She does not always say good things.'

'What sort of things?'

Tadeusz wriggled uncomfortably. He was really very thin, almost snuffed out by the Marks and Spencer sweater Rose had sent him a few months ago. 'It is still difficult to be a foreigner here and I do not think Mummy realizes.'

'But what is wrong with this Mrs. Mazi-Kazi — ?'

'Mrs. Kazimierska? Nothing. She is one of the pre-war people. But we'd better go up. Papa will be waiting for you.'

Six

BECAUSE Witold Rudowski admired Rose and wanted to interest her, he could only imagine doing this by telling her about his work. In fact there was little else he could talk about. He had always been too busy to go anywhere where opinions were exchanged. His only outside experience had been as a soldier in the war.

He had first spoken English with the girls in Manchester dance halls. At the back of his mind, unvoiced because there was absolutely nobody he could share it with, was the memory of those girls with the shoulder-length hair of the war years, the short swinging skirts and the wedge shoes. He had explored their soft bodies through interminable American patriotic films, *This is the Army, Two Girls and a Sailor, Up in Arms* (he remembered the titles because he was improving his English from them). Often he had held a blonde girl called Rose; for the last time, during a film in which the Andrews sisters, singing gamely, went down on a troopship torpedoed in mid-Pacific. He remembered that because the next day he broke his arm falling off a Bren gun carrier, and in hospital he met Janet. Later, when he was already engaged to Janet, Witek looked up the Manchester Rose again, but by then she was only interested in Americans.

Witek had no idea of the number of girls in England called Rose. It might be as frequent as ' Marysia ' here. The

little girl he came to know as Janet's sister was called Rose-
mary; it was only when she left school that she became
Rose.

Now, fresh from her walk, she came through the door of
his office, ushered in by Tadeusz, who once again made one
of his sudden disappearances. Rose and Witek were left
facing each other. There was always a lack of ease, something ponderous and embarrassing in his manner, but his
face shone with happiness.

'Here is where I work. I am afraid it is not up to the
standards of an English Speech Training Department. We
have to put up with what quarters we can get.'

Rose did not know what an English Speech Training
Department looked like. There were rows of dusty books,
mostly in late nineteenth-century bindings: dictionaries of
English place names, Anglo-Saxon texts, the works of the
English philologists, Skeat, Sweet and Weekley, whose very
names screech like chalk on a rough blackboard. A large
number of the books were in German.

'Those are from the library of the late Professor Roz-
wadowski. They are intended to form the nucleus of the
English Department's library.'

'They look rather old.'

'Yes, I don't think they will be very much use.'

'Does anyone read them?'

'No. But Mrs. Rozwadowska comes in and dusts them
from time to time. There is no room for them in her flat.'

'Doesn't anybody else come here?'

'You see we have no English Department in Biala Gora
yet. I am teaching students of history who must learn to
read books in English. Most of them have no interest but
some make good progress. We work together on tape and
with gramophone records.'

Two tape-recorders stood on a desk, one of the Russian type, in which the spools are one above the other, and an East German 'Smaragd'.

'Please sit down, Rose. Would you like some Nescafé?'

Witek came and sat on the desk opposite Rose. 'You must forgive me but this is rather a hobby horse of mine. You see, I know we could have a good English Department here. But there are many persons who do not want it. The professors of Russian and French are afraid English will become too popular. The professor of Comparative Philology thinks that no one should learn English without first having mastered Anglo-Saxon. Then they say I haven't the correct qualification. I have only a doctorate. But I have taught English all the time when nobody else did. Rose, you see I came back to Poland to do this. I am sure I could make a good department, perhaps the best one in Poland.'

He was carried away by his enthusiasm; he went over to the kettle and shook it fiercely to make it boil.

'For instance, I am in constant contact with Mr. Pilkington of the British Council and Mr. Golombek of the American Embassy. I think none of the English departments at the other universities avail themselves of such opportunities.'

He opened a drawer in his desk and showed Rose a pile of brightly coloured magazines. 'Mr. Golombek has sent these to me last week. *Holiday. Harper's Bazaar. Good Housekeeping. Screen World.*' He picked them up one by one and let them fall. 'I cannot lend them to students, of course, because they would sell them on the Black Market. Also I do not think the English style is a good one. Mr. Pilkington too has sent me several records by a composer named Vaughan Williams. Unfortunately we have not a suitable gramophone for these. But you see, they are ready to help.'

The kettle boiled and Witek mixed two cups of Nescafé. He stood close to her while she stirred and drank it. When he spoke of his ambitions the expression on his face was lively and attractive, though his breath was very bad.

'The Ministry of Higher Education, too. There my friend Mrs. Goldberg is very helpful and has good ideas. The Ministry supports me. It is the University that is against. The Rector wants a man who did philosophy and wrote his doctorial thesis on "Sir Gawain and the Green Knight". He lectures at Warsaw but most of the time he is a journalist. But his uncle is professor at Krakow and has many friends here. The students don't learn anything from him, but these people don't care about the students. The professors come into the room and deliver a lecture and go out again and do not know the name of any students. They leave the assistants to correct the examinations. So the students graduate without speaking the language. I am sure that this should not happen in Biala Gora. Here they must learn by the best modern methods.'

'What do people do who want to learn English now?' Rose asked.

'They must have private lessons. The younger generation — or, as we call it here, the new generation, the young people whose parents were not educated, they are anxious to learn. But now they are following other courses because there is no English course. And it is two years since the Ministry gave permission to start.'

'What will happen, do you think?'

'Nothing, while we have this Rector. He has five months more to serve. Then it will be too late for next year.' Witek stared into Rose's eyes. 'Rose, life has been very difficult for Janet and me. But I am sure if I can get this job everything will be all right.'

Confused by his vehemence, she turned away.

'Look, you haven't finished your coffee.'

'Sorry.'

'Now let me show you some things we have done.'

He opened the East German tape-recorder and switched it on. It hummed for a little, then spun to a halt, with the tape flapping frantically like a butterfly between two panes of glass.

'I must fix the correct tape, which will take about three minutes. Perhaps you would like to give me your opinion on this.'

He handed her a book. *First Moves in English* by Witold Rudowski, Doctor of Warsaw University. State Publishing House.

Rose opened a page at random. It was a reading text.

'In England and America the workers are working for the gain of capitalists or "bosses".[1] Only in the Peoples' Democracies do they get full value[2] for their work and share in all the benefits[3] that it brings.'

After all he had been saying, it was a little shock; almost as if a dirty postcard had been left in the book by mistake.

At the end of the exercise there was a list of questions:

1. What is it only in the Peoples' Democracies the workers get?
2. What is a 'boss'?
3. What has Dickens told us about the position of the English workers?

She closed the book and sat rather hopelessly with it on her lap. It was as though she had suddenly discovered Witek to be wearing a toupé.

'Of course there is a lot of things that may seem strange or perhaps silly to you. But I must put them in, in order for my book to be accepted by the State Publishing House.

Otherwise they would have the book done by a Miss Makula, a very nice lady who knows rather little English.'

'I see.'

He turned away, but worry was written all over the back of his threadbare suit. A moment later he faced her again.

'I am sorry, perhaps I give the wrong impression. I know now that it is not a good book. There are several errors in the treatment of the anomalous finites, for instance. But shall we say, it is better than any of the others?'

He turned to the tape-recorder and soon had it working again. 'Here we have the student who speaks and the teacher who corrects him.'

A voice said: 'The trees are greener since Easter.'

'The student,' Witek said.

There was more whirring but otherwise silence. Rose was apprehensive, for to her the voice had been unmistakeably Witek's.

Half a minute's silence told him something was wrong. He looked worried, then pressed the reverse button, and they started all over again.

This time the confusion was increased. Both voices were male, and Witek could not remember whether the teacher or the student had spoken first. Finally a female student took over. Now it was clear that Witek's was the better pronunciation, though by not very much. He was unusual among his compatriots in not having a musical ear.

Rose listened patiently through a series of exercises, until suddenly a girl's shrill voice broke in, there was an unidentifiable verse of 'Clementine', then a tempest of wild giggles.

Witek pressed the button hastily. 'That is nothing. We were having a little fun.' He quickened the speed and the whole tape ran through until the butterfly sounds started again.

'You can see, in any case, what we are trying to do.'

'It is very interesting.'

The girl's voice on the tape had infected Rose with a violent desire to laugh too, a thing which rarely happened when she was alone.

Seven

'**M**RS. BLAUT.'
        'Blaut.'
    'Miss Barcik.'
    'Barcikowna.'
    'There. And this is Miss Rose Nicholson whom we are all feeling we know so well already.'

The three women gleamed at Rose across the corner table in a crowded café. Rose did not like the unmixed company of women and seldom sought it if it could be avoided. She had come here for Janet's sake, as part of the balancing of favours to which the Rudowskis seemed to have committed her.

'Coffee? And cakes?' Mrs. Kazimierska asked. She waved for an elderly waiter who shuffled towards them.

'How do you like Poland?' Miss Barcik leaned forward with a helpful smile and a sudden access of blinking. The negotiation of unfair and leading questions was not a thing Rose was good at. She was about to plunge in, when Mrs. Kazimierska came to her aid.

'Come, come, Elzbieta, that is not a thing you must ask her, I know she is much too polite to tell us the truth. First she must try some of our very good cakes and then like silly women we will gossip about clothes and about people. Is that all right?'

41

Rose was as much put out by this as by the blinking woman's question.

They talked about clothes.

Though it was a weekday afternoon every table at the café was occupied and men with briefcases were waiting in the doorway for somewhere to sit down.

'Of course we are following all the fashions from the magazines you are sending to Janet.'

'And Janet, for you how is she looking?'

'She works too hard.'

Unlike Tadeusz, Mrs. Kazimierska was inclined to dismiss this. 'It is not so necessary, all this work. She is bad about asking enough money, our dear Janet. Look, I will tell you. A man goes to her and says: "I must learn English, I am going to Egypt, to Iraq, to Indonesia, please please teach me in three months, but I am so poor", and Janet believes him and takes him for nearly nothing. But we all know that man is an engineer making good money, more than any of us will ever see.'

'But she oughtn't to do that. Why don't you do something about it?'

'What can we do?'

'Can't you tell her who the people are when they come asking for lessons? Can't Witek tell her?'

It was the first time his name had been mentioned. The three round the table stiffened and the cake they were eating stopped dead in their mouths.

'Dr. Rudowski would think it beneath his dignity.'

'What do you mean?'

They looked at each other. Mrs. Blaut spoke first: 'Here we are all friends of Janet, you see.'

Rose examined her closely for the first time: a solid, handsome woman, by far the best dressed of the three. For her at least all the talk about clothes had not been academic. But, as happens when people speak a language with difficulty, her face was inexpressive.

'Yes?'

Mrs. Kazimierska patted Rose's hand. 'Hala means there are no secrets from us. What Janet has not told us we can guess. We all of us know Rudowski.'

From the gleams of accord in the eyes of the other two, you could see that they would not hesitate to go on. They did not know there could be such a thing as reticence. Whatever went wrong with anyone, however private or illicit the distress, they would be snuffling it out with the excited yelps of terriers.

'She hasn't told me anything,' Rose said.

Mrs. Kazimierska smiled fondly. 'You are so young, dear, but you can see when people are unhappy?'

'Well, perhaps they are not very happy.' She was going on to say that she could imagine how anyone could be very happy in Biala Gora. The three women, however, would feel this as somewhat near the bone. People like to tell you their misfortunes; they do not much like you to tell them.

'I've only been here one day. There's hasn't been time —'

Talking like this Rose was going along with them in the subject, assuming their possession of superior knowledge, which was flattering to them and also humiliating to her. She was hemmed in by the three intent faces, by Mrs. Kazimierska's huge nose, Miss Barcik's ceaseless blinking and Mrs. Blaut's solid calm. How well in fact did they know Janet? Were they fishing for more information?

She wished she could turn on them and tell them to shut up. But she was naturally without pugnacity and hated to be rude. Compared with them, too, she was over-armed with peace and security, and therefore crippled.

'And Tadeusz,' Mrs. Blaut asked. 'How do you find Tadeusz?'

'Oh really I —'

'He is a nice boy, very good-mannered. Rose — may we call you Rose — we always talk of you as Rose!'

'Oh, do.' She did not ask them their names nor wished to know them. To her they seemed infinitely old.

'I think Tadeusz is a little like you.'

'Oh surely not. I mean, he's so Polish, isn't he?'

'Not to us. To us he is very English.'

Rose felt a spark of excited hope flash through her: If Tadeusz is really English he can be saved from this after all, he can go away from all these people and never come back.

'He is not like Dr. Rudowski, I think,' Miss Barcik said. 'You went to the University this morning and he showed you his magnetogram — how it is in English?'

'Tape-recorder.'

'I think it is not very interesting. Hala, Krystyna and I, we are laughing at him for this. He is like a silly man with his little machines.'

'But everyone uses them now. I mean writers, actors, singers, all those . . . I know it's very boring when people turn them on at parties, and everybody thinks they ought to be funny into them. But if it helps people to learn English, why not have one?'

'It helps people to think Dr. Rudowski is important and up-to-date. We would all like to have magnetograms, it would impress very much our private students. But we cannot have them. But of course it is easy for him. He is on the right side. He has only to ask for things.'

'Elzbieta knows,' Mrs Blaut said. 'She works with him.'

'I am teaching English to economists and it is Dr. Rudow-

ski who looks after us poor teachers and tells us what we
must do. To mind our p's and q's, is that right?'

'Tell her about the system of marking.'

'Tell her how he changed the results of the examinations.'

'He does many things,' Miss Barcik said. 'But it is all
right for him. He is on the right side.'

'What do you mean, he is on the right side?'

'He is Party, *ma chère*,' Mrs. Kazimierska said.

'Oh, I see.'

'Of course we must understand that it was difficult for
him. Coming back from the West with an English wife. And
he wanted so much to be Professor of English.'

'He will be,' Mrs. Blaut said. 'He will be. His friends
will arrange that.'

Mrs. Kazimierska lit a cigarette in a little tube of red
glass. 'I do not think so. My great friend, Rektor Markiewicz says not. And Elzbieta's father is against him. There
are standards to be kept up, whatever people say. Even
Zwiersz agrees with that. Zwiersz is a very intelligent man.
Naturally Rudowski thinks that Zwiersz is on his side but
really he is not.'

'Who is Zwiersz?'

'He is one of the Deans of the University. He is the Party
man and deals with all that in the Dean's office.'

'Zwiersz is a friend of Adam Karpinski,' Miss Barcik
said.

'No, I do not think so.'

The names proliferated. Even with regard to Witek
Rudowski, their passion for gossip was hardly malice, but
an intense curiosity about people and motives, as though
these provided some energizing factor, some salt or spice
that their usual fare lacked. They rushed to a foreigner like
cats to catmint, yet at the same time could easily be dis-

tracted into speculations about anyone they knew of. The effect of their gossip was not trivial, but rather strong and stifling.

'If only Adam would come here, Mrs. Kazimierska said. 'He is so very clever. There is somebody for Rose to meet, a true Polish intellectual. His thesis was quite brilliant. They wanted to publish it in America. I read it, it was brilliant.'

'What was it about?'

'Sir Gawain and the Green Knight.'

'He was in Biala Gora last week,' Miss Barcik said. 'I saw him. Of course I did not speak with him. He was married to my cousin,' she told Rose. 'He was very bad to her and so we do not like him in our family.'

'Magdalena is a stupid girl. So, Adam was in town and he did not come to see me! I expect he was making intrigue. He must hurry up with it now. You see he is a great friend of Rektor Markiewicz and when *his* term of office is ended, there are no more chances for poor Adam in Biala Gora. But if he comes here again, Rose must meet him.'

'Do you think it is good?' Miss Barcik asked.

'Oh yes, he will like Rose. Forgive me, dear, but you are very like a Polish girl. You have not seen any of our pretty girls yet. They are lovely. Before 1956 they were not pretty, now they are pretty. In a year's time they will be ugly girls again, who knows?'

Mrs. Blaut said: 'No, they are always pretty. In the war, I remember that I say to head of Gestapo in Biala Gora: "No wonder your soldiers are liking so much our Polish girls. Your German men are handsome but your Frauen, so big and fat!" He laughed and agreed with me. He was not so bad, that one.'

'What was his name?' Miss Barcik asked.

'Fleischer.'

'Fleischer, ah, yes. I remember when they take over my father's flat. It was a beautiful flat, by the river — they dynamite it when they leave. My father said, where can we live? And Fleischer said, don't worry, you'll get a good flat. Then they cleared the Ghetto and we got a very good flat.'

Rose glanced quickly at Mrs. Kazimierska and Mrs. Blaut to see if there was any reaction to this. There was none.

'Rose must also meet her compatriot,' Mrs. Blaut said.

'I do not think she will find him interesting.'

'He is learning Polish with me. He is clever, but'— blinking furiously, Miss Barcik seemed about to commit a social indiscretion — 'I think we must take what he is saying with a pinch of salt. Is that correct?'

'Yes — I mean, I don't know. But why?'

'For instance he is saying he was at Cambridge. Evidently he is not *du monde*, indeed his parents are quite poor, he tells me. How can I believe that?'

'Believe what?'

'That he went to Cambridge. Only the well-born can go there, I think.'

Rose said: 'No, that's frightfully out of date. You see nowadays —'

While she spoke their mouths turned down. It appeared that they regarded this opinion as part of Rose's official instructions.

Miss Barcik laughed shortly. 'You see when you meet him. You will agree with me. He is a nice boy, but he is not always telling the truth.'

Rose said suddenly: 'Could I buy a bottle of vodka, do you think?'

'Not today,' Mrs. Blaut said.

'Why not?'

'Today is the day of paying wages. The drink shops are closed on such days. It is to prevent drunkenness.'

'One moment,' Mrs. Blaut said. 'You have dollars?'

'Pounds. At least, I've got one pound note with me.' Rose looked in her bag. 'Yes, here it is.'

'At Hoffman you can buy.'

'What is that?'

'Hoffman is the hotel. Now it is called "July Manifesto" but before the war it was Mr. Hoffman's and we still call it that.'

'Could I go there?'

'Of course,' Mrs. Kazimierska said. 'I'll take you, I live near there.'

Rose said goodbye to Miss Barcik and Mrs. Blaut without any particular wish to see them again. She greatly preferred Mrs. Kazimierska, though she knew now why Tadeusz had been so antagonistic to her. Mrs. Kazimierska had a certain detachment: the pleasures of gossip did not absorb her so completely as they did her friends. Rose was pleased that it was she who was walking with her through the twilit streets of Biala Gora.

The little shop windows were already lit, but most of them contained only scarlet and white decorations of crêpe paper, and framed portraits of Gomulka and Cyrankiewicz. The windows of meat-shops, however, displayed painted plaster models of legs of pork; inside, people were queuing for lengths of sausage.

Near the Hotel of the July Manifesto Mrs. Kazimierska said: 'Three years ago we were all too frightened to come here. It was only for foreigners and we did not want to be seen visiting them. And the staff were all U.B. Perhaps still are but they do not do anything now.'

She strode imperiously into the foyer, which was gloomy and unwelcoming with its heavy red hangings and varnished wood. A magazine stall stood beyond the reception desk, loaded with copies of *L'Humanité*, the *Daily Worker*, *Rude Pravo, Pravda,* and behind it were two showcases. One was full of folk art, dancing dolls with cretinous expressions and some lumpy embroidery which looked like kettle-holders; in the other there stood a display of bottles of vodka and the various cordials that are made from it. Everything was priced in dollars and cents.

Rose produced her passport, forms were to be signed in triplicate, she was sent twice to the reception desk and back again. She had to buy three half-bottles as they were not permitted to give change for her pound note. In the end, clutching her parcel triumphantly but with the grotesque vision of Miss Handisyde at the back of her mind, Rose said goodbye to Mrs. Kazimierska and took a taxi home.

Eight

ROSE unwrapped the bottles on the kitchen table. In the next room Janet was finishing an English lesson, the last of the day. Her voice sounded hoarse.

Rose looked into some drawers, could not find a corkscrew and pecked at the neck of the bottle with a fork. The little paper-wrapped cork slid out. She got a glass and poured herself a shot. By the time Janet came in, she was half-way through the second.

'Have some of this.'

'Darling, three bottles!'

'I need this, I can tell you. Your friends, I'm sure they're very nice and all that, but they're rather a lot for me to take, just at the beginning. They go on and on.'

'Hala and Elzbieta and Krystyna are the best friends I've got. They've always stood up for me.'

'I'm sure they have. They know far more about you than I do.'

'Rose, we know so little about each other at all.'

'I felt a terrible fool,' Rose said, turning away.

'You're tired, ought you to drink like that?'

'I told you I need it. Janet, I must ask you something. It's about Witek.'

'What about Witek?'

'Your friends talked about him like a sort of monster.'

The drink and her impatience made Rose exaggerate and dramatize.

'I see.'

'I like Witek. You didn't tell us much about him when you were in England. Only about Tadeusz.'

'We were taken up with Daddy, weren't we?'

'There was lots of time to talk, those last days. You could have told me about it then. I'd have understood. We'd always suspected, Daddy and I, but we didn't know for sure.'

'What *are* you talking about?'

'About Witek being a Communist.'

'Oh that. That doesn't matter at all.'

Rose was silent for a moment, wondering how to get to the point. 'It seems to matter, to your friends.'

'They're my friends, not his. I can't explain very well. Perhaps we'd better leave it till you know this place better.'

'Perhaps we'd better leave it.' Rose was being soothed down, and objected. 'If it doesn't matter, why won't you speak to him. It isn't very pleasant for me being in the house.'

'There isn't much Witek and I can discuss any more. We've been through it all. We look at things quite differently.'

'What about Tadeusz?'

'Especially Tadeusz.'

'But Tadeusz is all right, surely. So frightfully nice and intelligent. Honestly, I adore Tadeusz.'

'Perhaps you'd better take over from me, you seem to like everybody so much. Except for me. I seem to be the odd man out.'

'That's not fair. I'm trying to be helpful. All this makes it very difficult.'

'You can't help, Rose. You can't really.'

'Oh, I can. That's what you don't know.' Rose clutched Janet's arms excitedly, her eyes full of sparkle and distress. 'Only it's all going to be difficult.' She began talking very fast. 'You know last night I said I wanted to come here because I wanted to know about things here? You were hurt, you said you thought I wanted to visit you.'

'Yes.'

'Janet, I have got some exciting news. If I'd told you before I found this thing about Witek, something might have gone wrong.'

Janet sat down, huddled and tired. 'Tell me.'

'You remember about Aunt Louise?'

'Yes.'

'You know how she only wanted to leave her money to men, and when Nicholas was killed, our side of the family was out?'

'Yes, I know.'

'Well, she changed her mind. At least, she didn't really.'

'You mean, she left something to us?'

'It's a lot more difficult than that. She left it to Tadeusz.'

'Oh, my God. A lot of money?'

'Yes. A lot.'

Tears began streaming down Janet's cheeks. She sobbed and laughed. Rose could do nothing any more. She sat back exhausted on the divan, picking at the rough cloth under her fingers.

'It's all over then.'

'What's over?'

'This.'

Rose felt that for the last moments they had both been shaken, half-laughing and half-crying, on a large slightly out-of-control machine. Now she was worried that the shock might cause Janet to behave foolishly.

'We must be very careful to do the right thing.'

'When did all this happen?'

'She died just after Christmas. You remember, I wrote to you. I didn't say anything about what the solicitors told me. You know you said not to put important things in letters. I decided to give up my job and come here.'

'Otherwise you wouldn't have come?'

'Well, I don't know. Anyway, Micky was still around then. I told you about him. Actually, there was another thing.'

'Was there?'

'I was afraid to find you were unhappy. And not to be able to do anything about it."

'Unhappy! ' Janet laughed wildly. 'Just look at this flat. It took five years on a list to get it, and it's falling to pieces already. I've worked till I'm dog-tired every day. They're trying to take my own son away from me. You were afraid I might be unhappy.'

Rose was beyond listening to all this. Instead she thought of the complications ahead. Janet's whole life was disorganized by the news. Until some decision had been reached, there was a risk of more misery and even disaster.

'Aunt Louise was an old devil,' Rose said carefully. 'I expect she knew she was making difficulties. You must remember it's Tadeusz's money. What will he think about all this?'

'He's only a child.'

'It's his money. And in some ways it isn't a terrible lot.'

'If for years you've had nothing! Witek and I saved some money once and then they changed the currency and we lost it all. You'll never understand, Rose.'

'I mean, the money is not a lot if it is to help Tadeusz through his life. How's that to be done?'

Janet's silence showed that she had got the point. 'I see. Yes, it's going to be very difficult.'

'The boys are coming back for supper, aren't they? I don't think we should tell them yet.'

Janet nodded.

'It'll be a shock for Witek. I mean, he's after this job at the University, isn't he? And he's in with the Party, so he can't be expected to be pleased at the idea of his only son becoming a Capitalist.'

They both giggled at this. Janet said: 'Of course, it has nothing to do with him at all.'

'He controls Tadeusz's life.'

'I have no intention of telling him about it.'

The two women were a little drunk now, and exhilarated with dealing with something rather out of their depth. Their voices, chiming to a family tune of the upper middle class, rang out strangely through the dark, cramped flat. For them their grandparents would have expected marriage trusts and portions, but rising prices, the war and their father's career in education had made this impossible. Nevertheless both the sisters still thought and spoke about money in a way which was quite unknown in the city outside, where the native population had had a tradition of proud spendthriftness, of leaving commerce to the Jews and German merchants. Communism, which makes all financial values completely arbitrary, had only increased this.

What the men of the family would think, therefore, was uncertain. Rose remembered how Mark Tatham had warned her in Warsaw: money means such different things in different places.

Witek and Tadeusz could now be heard coming into the

hallway. Flushed, tipsy, the sisters embraced one another and prepared to tell lies.

Witold and Tadeusz were in the middle of an argument which did not break into English until they sat down at table. In this house, their language, with its slithery arcane noises, had become like a secondary sexual characteristic. It emphasized their privacy and separateness as men. You could as easily keep secrets from them as they from you: people can't guess thoughts in a foreign language, however well they speak it. Now, apart from their polite greetings, Tadeusz and Witek were too preoccupied to notice the suppressed excitement of the two women.

Tadeusz turned to Rose: 'It is not right. This teacher is giving us so much work for her class, we have no time for anything else. My colleagues wish to make a protest.'

'She is quite correct,' Witek said. 'It is in the syllabus. She will show you it.'

'Then we shall all fail.'

Witek said to Rose in his educational voice: 'It is difficult for him because many subjects are required. But he must do well. The number of students with secondary education increases every year and there is great competition for university places, especially for the courses he will follow.'

Rose tried to listen but she was watching her sister. There was a strange expression on Janet's face: she looked as if she was about to call Tadeusz back from somewhere he was going, but did not have the courage to raise her voice.

Tadeusz as usual ate ravenously, refused a second glass of tea and asked if he could leave.

When he had gone, Janet said: 'It's his health I worry about, with all this cramming and homework. A few years ago he had a spot on one lung. I sent him to the mountains at once, and it cleared up. But with this continual strain and being forced to keep up with others at all costs, you never know. There's a bad family history too, unfortunately.'

She fired a glance of hatred across the table and Rose saw Witek flinch from it.

Rose felt sad for him. He was not much as a man, but he had everything to lose, and he was going to lose it. After the giggling excitement of half an hour ago, Rose protested inwardly against these wrecking tactics, longing to blurt out the truth if only it would take away the stricken look from Witek's face. For the first time, Rose feared that Janet was a little crazy. She would use this good fortune, not for the calm and absence of desperation which a bank account was supposed to give you, but for revenge, to smash and destroy and create an unhappiness as fierce and broken as her own had been.

Nine

AFTER three days Rose began to move more easily in and out of the three rooms of the flat and the triangle of Rudowskis. There was still the discomfort of being accommodating instead of helpful, the slight ache of always feeling one is in the wrong chair, the hurry of shifting from room to room with the risk of leaving a pair of nylons, a half-finished detective story or a packet of cigarettes stranded, while the money-making activities of the house went on. The Rudowskis were furtive about these in a way strange to Rose, who had earned her own living since she was eighteen.

For the time being everything went on as usual. Neither of the sisters made any move towards confiding in Witold. Instead they bickered indecisively between themselves.

'I told the solicitors I'd find out what would be best for Tadeusz.'

'But it's so clear, isn't it?'

'Is it?'

'Rose, there are hundreds of people in Biala Gora who'd give their right hands to escape to the West. They are too proud to admit it to you. But I'll admit it because I happen to be one of them. Do you imagine I'd have come back in 1957 if it hadn't been for Tadeusz?'

'Why don't they go then?'

C

' Because they can't get passports. And *they* haven't any money.'

' That's older people. They want to be comfortable and there certainly isn't much of that here. But what about the young? I wouldn't want Tadeusz to end up like Mickey.'

' That's quite different,' Janet said impatiently.

' Mickey's Irish. They're supposed to be like the Poles. We must try and find out what's right. Not make him unhappy, too.'

' He's too young to know what he wants.'

' And Witek, too.'

' Him! '

On the fourth afternoon, Rose was cornered in the kitchen without cigarettes.

' Derek Loasby is on the telephone.'

' Who's he? '

' The Englishman at the University.'

' I remember. Your friend, the one who blinks, told me about him.'

She went into the other room and picked up the telephone. Janet's student, an elderly surgeon, was sitting on the divan breathing heavily just behind her.

' Yes? '

A hearty English voice went into some complex apologies and emerged with: ' I just wondered if you'd like to come out sometime and have a cup of coffee or something.'

' When, exactly? '

' Well, now.'

Rose glanced round her. The surgeon was staring politely ahead of him. The alternative to Loasby's invitation was the afternoon in exile, isolated in the kitchen. On the other hand the coat and skirt she would have to wear lay in the divan drawer underneath the surgeon. Already she seemed to feel his measured breath on her calves, urging her to decision.

'All right.'

'Shall I come and call for you?'

Janet and the surgeon were as motionless as waxworks.

'I'll find the place. Where is it?'

'The Kaprys. You were there with Miss Barcik.'

'I'll be about half an hour.'

Without looking round again, Rose snatched a packet of cigarettes from the table (these in fact belonged to the surgeon) and returned to the kitchen. Some time later she heard the surgeon leave. She went through to retrieve her coat and skirt before Janet's next pupil arrived.

'I must say I haven't found that young man very friendly considering we were the only two English here. I could have given him a lot of tips. But he goes off on his own and nobody seems quite to know what he gets up to.'

'Perhaps I'll find out.'

'Did you remember your key? I've got my class at the Engineering Institute this evening.'

Ten

IN the café where Rose had sat with Janet's friends, the first room was quite full and there was no sign of anyone who looked English. She headed through the tobacco-smoke and smell of old clothes into a larger room beyond. Here faces were thrust forward at each other over the wet-ringed tables, tongues loosened not by drink but the urgency of getting their say. On a yellow brown dais ornamented with plywood cut-outs of lyres, a violinist and a pianist were performing. Above them hung a sort of mosaic relief, representing a huge-footed woman carrying sheaves of wheat.

The girl saw a hand shoot up, followed by a young man in a tweed coat.

'I daren't leave here, someone will grab the table,' he shouted to her, and indeed at his first movement two stout surly men carrying plastic briefcases pushed Rose aside and made towards it. One of them seized hold of the chair Derek Loasby was keeping for Rose. Loasby got it away from him by force.

'Sit down on it quickly.'

She did so, feeling herself used as a weapon in their conflict. The men moved off, scowling, between the tables.

'They're so predictable, the Poles. Hospitality at home and awful manners in public.'

Rose looked doubtful at this generalization, which was

perhaps only occasioned by the pomposity of nervousness. She hated the starts of conversation, 'drawing people out' as though they were to be extracted from holes: they had far better stay where they were.

As soon as she could, she took a careful look at Derek Loasby. His hair was dark red, his nose another shade of red and some pimples along his neck, made by a dull razor-blade, were nearly purple. A fall of dandruff lay on the rough tweed of his collar.

'Coffee? It's not bad here, compared with the other places.'

He would keep shifting around in his seat. These movements, which were constant with him, did not indicate any particular excitement, nor were the questions he now fired at the girl evidence of any real curiosity. He was too full to the brim with himself for that.

In the end he got hold of a waiter, a surviving pachyderm from the days before the war, whose mournful appearance was enough to make even Loasby reject the pretence, often helpful with girls, that he was a *habitué* of the place. Instead he quite competently ordered two large coffees.

'It's jolly nice seeing someone English again. I love it here, of course. But you can't go around saying that to people. They don't even like you to, for one thing.'

'Surely some people like to hear nice things?'

'Party people. They've no time for us, we're the decadent Westerners. Jolly good fun, too. Some people say to me, why didn't you go to Warsaw or Krakow, more going on. I like it here. Do you know, I've been the only English person here this winter.'

'There was my sister.'

'British wives don't really count do they? Sorry, is that rude?'

' I suppose so. I don't know really.' Rose was not really attending to what he was saying, being put off by the pugnacity of his approach. He was half-way over the little table; he had adopted from the natives the tactic of close breathing, even the direct stare into the shrinking pupils. He only drew back when the waiter placed two glasses of muddy-looking coffee between them.

' Put the sugar in and then the saucer on top. The theory is the grounds go down.'

They emptied the little bowls of grey sugar on to the bubbling surface of the coffee. Rose burnt her fingers trying to get at the saucer under the scalding glass.

' Here, take my hanky.' He produced something stuck together and sooty.

' No, thank you.'

At this rate it would take half an hour to drink the coffee and he was pushing nearer.

' I wanted to ask you. We meet up, me and my friends, every Saturday. We dance at the Students' Club. How about it? '

Rose did not bother to hide the effort of reaching a decision on this. She did not even pretend that she had not understood, as one often did on receiving an invitation that might be unattractive.

Though callow, Loasby was not stupid. A moment of pure misery made him tremble: he had overshot the mark with someone who was really worthwhile.

' All right,' Rose said.

A smile of relief shone all over his face. It would not stop, it went on and on.

Rose smiled back.

' Jolly good. I'm sure you'll like this place we go to. They've got a very good jazz group. There's a lot of good

things about this country when you know your way around.
And, with parcels, there's very little you can't get.'

'What parcels?'

'You have them sent from England. Nescafé, aspirin,
things like that. Ball-point pens. You haven't any ball-point
pens, have you?'

'I've got one but I use it.'

Now he had started to press his foot against hers. The
girl retreated. She hit an unexpected leg of the modernistic
table, and their coffee slopped over.

'That's a pity.' He was still talking of the ball-point pens.
'You could have some sent, couldn't you? Though through
the post you might have to pay duty. Nescafé is better. I've
got friends who'll take anything like that off me. I sold
some clothes before I went to Vienna at Christmas and
stocked up again there.'

'How did you get the money out?'

'Easy. I took a Russian camera and sold it.'

He had got carried away again. He shot a panicky
trapped look at the surrounding tables. There was no sign
that anyone had understood a word he was saying, but
should there have been? He gulped turned pinker and was
silent for a moment. Miss Barcik had hinted that Loasby
told lies; in fact his stumbling candour was so obvious that
it was quite unrecognizable to anyone not accustomed to
the English.

'I — I must say I've met an awfully nice lot of people.
There's this girl, perhaps I oughtn't to mention her name
just now' — he gave another glance at the grey men surrounding them — 'You'll meet her on Saturday. And the
others, too. Everyone here is really sociable.'

'It's surprising, isn't it, when they all live so close
together.'

'Perhaps that's just it. If you've never been lonely you never want to be alone.'

'What happens if you can't stand the people you live with?'

'That's too bad.' His face drew nearer again. 'In London if you're young and poor you can have a horrible time. They said: "Join the Young Conservatives". Well I did and all the girls were plain and the lads just as desperate as me. No help at all. Coming here was a revelation, I can tell you.'

There was a sort of wet film on his eyes; pity for himself.

Somewhat repelled, she said: 'But you only have a nice time because you're English. What if you were a Pole?'

He leaned back in his chair and put his thumbs in the armholes of his pullover. 'I'm sure I'd have an even nicer time.'

'This is a wonderful country,' he added in a loud voice, looking furtively round him.

This seemed to leave them much where they were before.

Eleven

WHILE Rose had coffee with Loasby, Witold Rudowski was sitting at home with a pile of language tests in front of him. Outside the walls and windows of the opposite block shone with the melancholy light of a late spring evening; inside the flat, it was already dark.

Witek was unable to work. Two or three times his impatience at himself brought him to the window: the mere sight of other people, the representatives of mass society, might remind him of his duties towards them.

The janitor's children were playing in the dust under the walnut tree. Three young men who had acquired shares in a motor-cycle were engaged in roaring the engine up and down. And now the lame ex-soldier had gone to let out his tumbler pigeons. Five of these flew up on to the roof opposite, where they fussed and shimmered in a black and white group. Then, when the soldier called them, they fluttered down one by one, performing on the way a complete back-somersault in the air, and alighted inside the walnut tree, which was still leafless. The pigeons stayed there, dark fruit-shaped objects against the bright sky.

Motor-cycles and pigeons were cures for the depression and anxiety caused by the blunt resistance of the physical world. This seemed not to obey his compatriots as it did the Germans and the British. Witek's cure was skiing, in which nothing whatever got in his way. But now the hills

nearest Biala Gora were bare except for little corners of old
snow among the spruce trees. You had to go to the Tatry, a
hundred and fifty miles away, for good skiing at this time
of the year.

Dreaming of mountains, Witek went back to the language
tests.

Each period of his life had presented him with immediate problems which must be solved before he could move
on. Like most conformists, he had no resonance. He bored
others because of his lack of feeling for the past; he never
joined in those impassioned conversations by which Poles
recapitulate their country's history and increase the unease
of their destiny. Up till now his hopes had been limited
and precise.

The shock had come the moment he saw Rose's luggage:
two suitcases of brown pigskin, the smaller one having zip-
fasteners. She had bought them for this visit and because she
had travelled by air they were still unbattered. They smelt
new.

As such things will, however much we tell ourselves they
are evidence of no importance, the suitcases represented all
the difference between his life and the life of somebody who
might have a chance of possessing Rose. You couldn't get
anything so completely achieved as those suitcases here. Not
a pair of scissors nor a vacuum cleaner nor a decent meal:
they all had something wrong about them, some immediate
defect or built-in drawback. Increased prosperity would
never change this. Officially he considered it unfortunate
that people here attended church so assiduously, but the
churches were the last places where, among properly made
things, actions were properly performed.

And so even in Rose's absence, Witek was disturbed,
steeling himself not to look at the frail tangle of her nylons

across a chair, her underclothes innocently hanging up to dry in the kitchen. These extensions of Rose into the surrounding area were what made her remarkable. Here nobody's possessions had any personality any more, so that where you lived became no more informative than the mark of your head on the pillow. Rose's irritating untidiness made her always present.

He could escape to the University; there his tape-recorder was waiting to be played with, papers were ready to sign and useful little conversations happened in corridors. But this afternoon by chance he was alone at home. Tadeusz was at a school meeting: he was his class representative on the committee dealing with summer excursions. Janet at the Engineering Institute was giving one of her evening classes.

Giving up the attempt to work, Witek lay on the trestle bed which stood among his bookshelves. He yawned and stretched in the way people have whose fantasies are too much for them. Then he dozed off.

He woke to hear someone coming into the flat.

'Tadeusz?'

Rose stood in the doorway.

'You've been asleep,' she said.

He sat up, confused. 'Impossible to work. A slight headache.'

'Shall I make tea or something?'

Waking reality descended on him like a cloak of lead. His tongue fumbled with the stiffness of the English language, which so often seemed to paralyze a small section of his brain. He could never manage to say quite what he meant but always something ponderous and banal. He had hardly realized this before and it would not have mattered with anyone else but Rose.

'I help you,' he said, 'Rose.'

They stood on either side of the kitchen table. Against the drumming of tap-water into the kettle, Rose said: 'I've been meeting the local Englishman.'

'I hear he is very nice.' In fact, he had heard of nothing but suspicions and pertinent questions.

'No, not really. Rather stupid.'

Witek laughed nervously, a little appalled that she should criticize one of her countrymen to him so brusquely. Giving opinions about other people was betraying them a little: it was not to be done without a painful sense of duty.

Rose lit the gas. 'I want to find out things and he obviously doesn't know the right answers.'

'Please? To find out things?'

'Yes. Witek, what do *you* think is going to happen here?'

'Please?'

'Is life going to get any better?'

'But life is getting so much better every day. Sometimes we must be wondering, can it be true?'

'I suppose so. Are you happy? I know it's an awful thing to ask.'

'We have our work. Janet has her work. I have my work.' It sounded like an exercise in the Simple Present Tense. 'This is not perhaps interesting for you. But—I feel I am doing good.'

'I'm sure you are.' Rose said, slightly repelled. 'But what about Tadeusz?'

'He is an ambitious boy.'

'Can he do any good here? Would he be better off in England?'

'I cannot tell. Remember, he is a Pole—I do not hear very good accounts of Polish people in England.'

How impossible it was! All that one might offer Tadeusz, perhaps holidays abroad, perhaps an English University, the freedom to go anywhere he liked for a few years, would mean nothing at all to Witek.

'But wouldn't you like him to travel abroad?'

'Here we cannot get money for foreign travels. Only for scientific workers. There is not foreign currency.'

'They use that as an excuse. In the West, even the poorest students go. They just go. Why can't Tadeusz?'

Witek looked pained. She was attacking him. What good would it do him to agree with her, merely to join in her mood?

'He would waste a lot of time from his studies and the others would be in front of him.'

She turned away, defeated. Witek watched her, with hurt love in his gaze. Any relationship with someone who disapproved of him as much as Rose did could only be painful. Mentally he tried saying goodbye to her, in the same way that Janet was always saying goodbye to Tadeusz: they existed in another world, into which they could not be followed. But, like Janet, he could not quite give up hope.

When Rose faced him again, she was fierce.

'If you could leave Poland, would you?'

'No,' he shouted back. 'Of course not.'

After this, they both faltered.

'Do forgive me asking, Witek. You know, with Janet and everything, I can't help thinking about it.'

'I understand.' He frowned. 'I cannot know what Janet tells you. I know she is not happy.'

'Well, I —'

'I know,' he said, more loudly. 'But perhaps we are not all to blame. This is new, since she was in England. Before that, life was very hard for us and then she was wonderful.'

'She thinks Tadeusz is missing something.'

'I understand. You think so, too.'

'I don't know. But I must find out.'

'Why must you find out?'

Rose made the tea with a good deal of fuss and then said: 'Because I'm fond of you all and at the moment I don't have anyone else I much care for, that's all.'

It was enough for him. He was perplexed by their whole conversation: half-scared and half-flattered, like a hired guide whom lady tourists suddenly ask a lot of personal questions.

Rose poured two glasses of tea. 'Here you are.'

'There isn't lemon, I am sorry.'

'Do you have lemons here?'

'There were some about three weeks ago. I could get two for Janet. She was keeping them for something and they went bad.'

'Poor Witek.'

He frowned, stirred his tea and handed her back the spoon.

Then he looked quickly down into his glass. The warmth in his eyes was not only from the tea. Again he had noticed her nightdress hanging on the line behind her. It was all frills and ridiculousness and it made him want to cry. With anguish he imagined Rose's flat in Kensington, a place where she was not merely represented by a nightdress or a crumpled stocking, but extended to pictures and furniture and a bed. A bed which was not folded up before breakfast, but existed in all its flagrancy throughout the day. He had covertly examined the pictures of such beds in the magazines which Rose sent to Janet.

'You asked me if I leave Poland. I did not say clearly what I mean. Later, if I get the post of head of the English department, I wish very much to re-visit England. In one year, perhaps.'

'That would be lovely.'

He stared across, deep into her eyes, then looked away. 'You will be in London?'

'I don't know. Probably. What about Tadeusz?'

'Tadeusz?' He was puzzled.

'Witek, why don't you let Tadeusz come to England for a little while. I'd pay his fare and put him up and I know some children of his own age who'd love to show him round.'

'Tadeusz?'

'Yes. I want him to come — on a visit.'

'But why?'

'Just so that he can see England.'

'That is not possible.'

'Why not? It'd be such fun.'

'It is not possible.'

'I don't see why. I mean, if he can get a passport and everything.'

'It would disturb him in his school work.'

'All right, for a short time only. In the holidays.'

'No. I cannot allow it.'

Suddenly she was sick of him. She moved off to the sink, showing an impatient back.

He watched her for a moment and then realized that she was not going to speak to him again. She was sulking, as Janet did. Neither of them wanted anything to do with him, only with Tadeusz. He put down his glass, began to say something but the numb feeling of speaking English lay over his brain again.

Yet he could not leave her thinking ill of him. 'Rose.'

'No, it's no good. You've told me it's no good.'

'It is not me but —'

'It is you. Other people go.'

'No, you do not understand. Things are not so easy for me. In any case, it is too late to apply for a passport. That takes four or five months.'

Rose counted quickly on her fingers. 'July, August — say the end of August. There'd be time.'

'Perhaps.'

'Witek, do let him come. He'll love it.'

'You have not spoken with him about this?'

'No, but I will. He'll persuade you, I'm sure.'

'Please not. Do not speak. It will disturb his work. Although he complains of his courses he is a very diligent boy.'

'He can't apply for a passport without knowing it, can he?'

'I will see first what may be done.'

'You'll let him apply. Oh, Witek, thank you.'

'No. Well, perhaps.'

He had never seen her look so happy before. Since her arrival she had been cast down, not only by the way in which she found them living but by the muted sadness which lay over everything in Biala Gora.

'Yes?'

'I promise nothing. But there is a chance.'

He shivered, feeling he had bartered something away for nothing, or for nothing more substantial than a frilled nightdress on a hanger. Later, when he was alone, he would run his face across it.

Twelve

ROSE was delighted at what she had gained. Once she had got his confidence, she thought, Witek would accept her judgment on a good deal more. And that night, before they went to bed, she told Janet.

'He said Tadeusz could come to England this summer.'

'Oh, darling.'

'All very secret, of course. He doesn't want me even to tell Tadeusz yet.'

'Then I'll tell him.'

'Please don't. You'll make my position very difficult. I'll have to make all sorts of promises, of course, about looking after him and sending him back in time for the school year.'

'Of course.'

'But it's what we want, isn't it? We want Tadeusz to be able to choose his life.'

That night Rose's elation was so great that she did not notice that Janet was scarcely enthusiastic. But by the following morning Janet had evidently changed her mind. With the replete looks and shared glances of those who are keeping secrets, the sisters watched Tadeusz eat his breakfast. It was as much as they could do to stop touching him the whole time.

As he devoured his scrambled eggs Tadeusz was conscious of something going on behind his shoulders. He judged it to be one of those female mysteries which adolescence had made him confident to dismiss. He smiled tolerantly to them both, swallowed a second cup of coffee and prepared to leave. They kissed him, seeing him off out of their immediate love with a sense of relief.

Janet had only three pupils on Saturday and the rest of the day she wandered round absent-mindedly attending to the flat, humming bits of dance-tunes that dated from the war years. She was much nicer to Rose, who began to regret Derek Loasby's invitation and the prospect of a student's Saturday evening.

While Rose was changing to go out, Krystyna Kazimierska arrived. Janet went to make tea, and Rose, too, was retreating into the kitchen. The other stopped her, and sat admiring her clothes while she changed. She made little appreciative noises at Rose's underwear.

' How is Janet? '

' Much more cheerful,' Rose said, without equivocation.

' I am so happy. It is a wonderful thing to have you here. But Rose, when are you starting to see the rest of our country? My sister has written from Krakow saying you may go there whenever you like. She has the room empty because her daughter is abroad.'

In the stress and complications among the Rudowskis, Rose had forgotten she was here disguised as a tourist; everyone expected her to go away from Biala Gora at some time or other.

' I'd love that.'

' She has many friends who would take you around Krakow. Here there is nothing for tourists to see.'

' I suppose not.'

' She doesn't speak English. But you can speak French with her.'

Janet, humming 'You are my sunshine' came back with tea. Mrs. Kazimierska watched the two sisters intensely. She caught Rose's eye and seemed to be signalling indecipherable messages, perhaps about Janet. Rose was being asked to take part in one of those Slav bouts of feeling, so strange to the Anglo-Saxon, in which sympathy goes mounting up to the point of explosion, after which any indifference looks like betrayal.

There was no doubt, however, about the change in Janet. She swirled airily between them and when the bell rang she ran to it with a stagey lightness.

'Oh, do come in. You are a stranger. It's really quite an honour for us isn't it? I'm sure you're so busy.'

At the doorway, Derek Loasby eyed Mrs. Rudowska with distrust. Though he still shifted from one foot to the other with his usual suppressed excitement, he was still contrained and embarrassed when he greeted the other two.

'Now do tell us what you've been doing,' Janet went on. 'We're fascinated to know, simply fascinated.'

He blushed. What was the hag up to? His confidence waned; he suspected he was being teased. He muttered something about learning the language.

'Try some out on Mrs. Kazimierska and me. Oh, please do!' She clasped her hands to her breast, pleading.

Loasby looked at Rose but she was offering no help. He toyed with the idea of an obscenity he had just learned, but was scared of the formidable Mrs. Kazimierska.

She rescued him. 'Elzbieta Barcik says he is very good. But he speaks Russian, I think.'

'Yes, I learned it at the University.'

'Oxford or Cambridge?' Janet asked.

'London, actually.'

'Oh, I see.' She looked at Rose with a twinkle.

Loasby stood frowning, unable to understand what was going on. Perhaps Mrs. Rudowska had heard some scandal about him and he was unwelcome. With an effort he tried being less self-conscious, and decided that she might be drunk.

Rose said: 'We ought to be going.'

'Yes, they'll be waiting for us.'

In the hallway, surrounded by bicycles and packing cases and skis, he helped her on with her overcoat.

'Just a moment. I'd better take my key.'

Rose, too, was surprised and worried by Janet's behaviour. Perhaps this was how middle-class women had spoken in the thirties; how their mother, as housemaster's wife, had dealt with the parents of boys she considered common. Or perhaps Janet had learned it at a military hospital, from some snobbish matron roaring through the menopause. It was a folk memory preserved through years of Communist exile, a faded wreath from the bourgeois world.

Loasby heard Rose's voice raised in anger. Her sister answered: 'Why should he get away with it, a little oik like that?'

Rose came back. She did not speak but pushed her chin right down into her coat collar. She took his arm as they walked to the tram stop.

When they were in the tram she said: 'I'm sorry about that.'

'Don't give it a thought.'

'No, I must. I think living here turns some people mad.'

'What's an oik, anyway?'

'It's — it's a slang expression. From the war, I think.' She stared out at the dark blocks of buildings and the empty streets.

'You have to be tough living here, that's all.'

'Why should anyone *have* to be tough,' she complained. 'It's awful isn't it?'

Loasby was silent: the Spartan atmosphere was one of the things that attracted him, though it would be impossible to explain it to her.

They had forgotten to pay their fares. The conductress now stood between them, in a coat of rough sheepskin and with a face of Mongolian impassivity.

'She's tough all right.' He handed over two coins. '" What breath blew out the light within that brain?"'

'What's that?'

'From a poem. I can't remember which,' he added awkwardly, though he could.

'Oh.'

'Some people have still got the lights in their brains all right, I can tell you. You just follow me.'

Thirteen

THE whole centre of Biala Gora, including the mediæval market-place and the Town Hall, was destroyed by the Germans during their retreat in 1945: a centre of Germanic culture could not be allowed to fall into the hands of Slav barbarians. The Polish authorities, when they re-occupied the city, were in some doubt about restoring it in a style which had never been Polish. But evidently these conflicts of opinion had now been overcome. The gables of merchants' houses were beginning to take shape behind a maze of scaffolding. The Gothic Town Hall was already completed and its cellar had been handed over to the Students' Union. Soon the market-place of Biala Gora would be a place for tourists to visit. Its years as a mass of rubble would scarcely be referred to: it would be first new, then old, all over again.

Derek Loasby led Rose Nicholson across the cobbles to the portico of the Town Hall. While they waited to be let in, music and light were welling up out of a grating at their feet.

A small plump girl with crew-cut hair was the first to greet them. Derek biffed her confidently on the behind. 'This is Wanda. She doesn't speak any English, in fact we don't let her. Her job is to help me with my Polish. I wonder what's happened to old Mirek. *Gdzie jest Mirek?*'

The girl shrugged her shoulders and continued to stare

78

blankly at Rose. Three other girls left their friends and gathered to inspect Rose. Loasby greeted them all. This, then, was the explanation of his bouncy happiness: here he crowed and strutted in triumph. He had found a place where neither his spectacles nor his manner nor the recrudescent boil-crop on the nape of his neck made any difference; a place where, as now, some incomprehensible mistake in his use of the language roused a conjoint peal of laughter; where he could be a joker without ever making a joke.

Half-hidden by the massive pillars that supported the vaults. five young men sat on a platform playing jazz. Abstract paintings hung on the whitewashed walls, amateurish and probably self-mocking, as though whoever painted them had not considered them anything more than a necessary gesture for the place and the time. Everything here was a gesture, the jazz, the pictures, the Western clothes and hairstyles. In recent years such things had become officially tolerated but somehow unrenewable. The students, however, were always being renewed and nearly a whole University generation had passed since the October revolt. Some of the faces in the cellar had the candour of those to whom everything here was still exciting. They had the rare charm of the young who do not pretend they have seen and done all this before, and their liveliness made you happy to look at them.

Derek gave Rose a glass of Jugoslav wine. 'I can't think what's happened to old Mirek.'

In the presence of his friends, he backed away from her a little and she was left isolated with the glass of wine, trying to make it last, while the girls waited for her to manifest herself in some typical way or other. The blank-faced Wanda even came up and fingered the woollen dress Rose was wearing, at which the small group was rocked by giggles. But no conversation ensued.

After another conference with Wanda, whom Rose was beginning to regard with some antipathy, Derek asked Rose to dance. On the little dance-floor their progress was halting, because the jazzmen's intense attitude to their task led them into self-intoxicated 'breaks' of great complexity. Everyone stood still and listened. During one of these interludes a tall man, with short blond hair brushed forward, came and stood beside them. He placed a large hand on Derek's shoulder. Derek flushed with pleasure. His face always transmitted everything he was thinking.

'Miroslaw Sypniewski.'

The young man bowed and brought his heels together. He kissed Rose's hand.

'This is Mirek. He speaks perfect English. Our worries are over. Let's all go and have a drink.'

The three of them sat at a small table to drink more of the mouth-drying red wine.

'This character here, honestly, I can tell you it was quite something to discover him in a town like this. He's the perfect introduction to life here. If you want to know absolutely anything, Mirek's your man. Yes, sir. He's a real fixer. Correct?'

The newcomer did not answer. He flicked sly, rather small green eyes from one to the other, while his meaty hands were crumpled in front of his face and his body was shaken by the unvoiced giggles and breathy grunting noises which Poles emit at times of surprise and amusement.

'But you're a student, aren't you?' Rose did not want either of the young men too sure of themselves.

'Yes, I study Sanskrit.'

'Oh.'

'One must continue to be a student, it is much the best way to live. The Sanskrit course is rather a long one. Perhaps also I am often failing in the exams.'

'He thinks they'll take his scholarship away,' Derek said helpfully.

'At present that does not much matter if I may stay at the University. You see, I earn by giving lessons in English. Perhaps my English is not good enough but I must work.'

He presented this as his fate: he did not think he should. With his height and looks, there was about him certainly a sort of damaged authority, as though fallen from antediluvian glory; this separated him from the others in the place who were dressed, like him, in dirty black sweaters and tubular trousers.

Derek, who was staring at them both with the pleasure of the successful go-between, now became conscious of the girl Wanda standing at about three yards distance. He shifted around undecidedly, then left them.

For a while Mirek was silent, with a stillness not of timidity but of speculation. He did not look at Rose; he was absorbing her presence by a kind of mental deep-breathing.

When at last he spoke, he was still formal. 'I am told this is like a *cave* in Paris. You think so?'

'Oh no.'

'The students will be disappointed to hear that.'

'The faces are quite different here. More hopeful.'

'Is that so? I wonder why?' He looked behind him at the dancing couples as though he expected to see something different. 'They must be very stupid then. What can they be hopeful about?'

'Perhaps they are glad to be students. Perhaps they wouldn't have been students before the war.'

'And now they are students what can they hope for? What can I hope for? Please tell me.'

She laughed. 'You tell me. I've only been here a week.'

'I can tell you. I hope for nothing at all.'

Against the blank stare with which he said this, she was silent, but since Mirek belonged to a class or a way of life which might sooner or later include Tadeusz, she felt concerned and interested.

The music stopped. Derek relinquished his partner, and came back to the table.

'Why aren't you dancing? Slackers! '

'Would you like to dance? '

'Not really,' Rose said. 'Please go on about the students.'

'What's all this about the students? I think they're terrific.'

Mirek looked at Derek with tolerance. 'For Mr. Loasby it is very good here because of the vodka and the nice Polish girls. But Polish people are always taking this for granted even in the worst times. Not like England where you have Puritanism and are against pleasure.'

Derek nodded vigorously but Rose said: 'That's not really true, you know.'

'I think so. My uncle was there in the war.'

'Things have changed.'

'Perhaps.' Rose had got to know that this word expressed strong disbelief. 'But in Poland we have drink and making love all the time. We are always looking for something which our history will not give us. We will never get it and so I think the students are stupid to look hopeful.'

'Would you leave here if you could? '

Derek looked embarrassed at this. His eyes fled from one to the other. Mirek blew out smoke and said: 'I cannot ever leave Poland.'

'Why not?'

'Because I was in prison.'

Rose blushed. For her the word connected still with guilt. 'I'm sorry.'

'Don't mention it.' He smiled crookedly. 'That is why I am older than the other students. I did not really fail some examinations.'

'Oh, good.'

She wondered what it was correct to think, and what Derek thought. If Mirek was really his friend, he must condemn this iniquity in a place he so much approved of. But perhaps the lurid fact of gaol gave Mirek an added attraction.

'You see why it is better for me to live here than Warsaw. In winter I am giving English lessons to my colleagues and in summer I am taking foreign visitors round factories. I am a very good guide. I have all of statistics at the tip of my tongue. I know where the canteen will be built and the washroom and the flats of workers. I know the production figures for next year—'

'But not last year?'

'Next year is so very much better. I tell the visitors all that and they are much interested. They return to their countries pleased and frightened a little, which is a nice feeling to have.'

'Why can't you tell them the truth? They'd be just as interested.'

'This is my job. I do not wish to go back where I came from just because I tell two Dutch journalists or an English Trades Unionist something they are incapable to understand. However they try, if they try till they explode, they will never understand what it was like living under Hitler and Stalin and what it is going to be like again. This is like talking through a wall of glass. Even if our factories will work just as well as yours, do you think the wall of glass will go away?'

'I suppose not,' Rose said. 'All the same, if you won't tell the truth to Dutch journalists, how do we know you tell it to us?'

Derek squirmed again at this, but almost at once, another of the girls appeared beside him. Mirek watched them go, laughed to himself, and then turned again his look of absorptive charm.

She was not going to be put off. 'Well, suppose you do tell us the truth, why?'

'Derek is my friend. He must learn.'

'And me?'

'You are involved a little, I think. You have relatives here. You are not dangerous.'

Rose finished her glass of wine. 'Life here doesn't look the same to everyone, you know.'

'I know, I know.' It was something he had heard too often before. He held up a large hand, placatory but at the same time repressive. 'People forget. Or they are too young, they have nothing to compare. I am old enough. I remember how we found one day that the whole world had turned grey, grey streets, grey houses, grey faces, grey girls. The war didn't do that and statistics will not change it. Stalin did it. It was like a bomb. It was his fall-out. We are trying to tidy up but the greyness has got into everything. I will fetch another drink.'

She watched Mirek return with two brimming glasses. In front of him the crowd separated without being asked to: you realized that in the most democratic society people must be born knowing where to put their hands and feet, possessing grace, this word for a physical thing which has always the shadow of a religious meaning.

Rose's brother Nicholas had possessed it, and now perhaps Tadeusz. But the ambitious ones are people like Witek Rudowski who have always to struggle to make the events of a year or a moment turn out correctly.

Arguing from Witek's side, Rose said: 'My nephew is going to be an engineer. Surely he won't see everything grey?'

'Don't you know what a dictatorship means?'

'You think nobody can be happy. But I think he can be.'

'Who?'

'My Polish nephew,' she said patiently. She wanted him to agree with her about something, it did not matter what. His reckless way of talking had been intended to attract her, and perhaps had done this, but it really was not worth his while to put himself into danger.

'I think he can be happy,' she said again.

'In the mountains. The first time he has a woman. When he gets really drunk at somebody's name-day party. Is that enough? Perhaps for the English. We had better ask Mr. Derek.'

Loasby was jigging past them with a third girl. His forelock was flapping up and down and his face was radiant. It was difficult not to take him as an example of someone falling into exactly the place intended.

Rose agreed with Mirek: she wanted more than that for Tadeusz. For the last moments she had been thinking of Tadeusz here in three years' time as one of these students, even as Mirek perhaps. But, with Tadeusz's chances of escape, would anyone here have chosen this? Almost certainly not. But would they have been right?

Mirek watched her perplexed face. 'Well?'

'I think you're very depressing.' The inadequacy of this

remark emerged charming and shrill. He accepted it with glee.

Rose's attempt at optimism had been exactly what he wanted. She realized this now. The sort of things you could say, the sort of answers it was incumbent on you to make were drastically limited. In the end from courtesy and kindness you were the sort of person they wanted you to be. You kept their argument going by always losing it.

'Let's go away from here,' he said. 'Let's go for a walk.'

'All right.'

They left. They did not say goodbye to Derek.

Fourteen

THE nights are quiet in Biala Gora, which then enters the pre-industrial age. Even on Saturday nights the drunks, though ragged and fierce, are quiet as they stumble along in their happiness. A faint light hangs over the factories and occasionally blue flashes from the tram wires illuminate the lower sky, but otherwise it is very dark. When a horse and cart go by the hoofbeats echo into completely empty streets. Few people hear them. In grim last-century houses the inhabitants lie packed together in exhausted sleep, three and four to a room.

Rose and Mirek walked away from the Town Hall, rather separated and pacing rhythmically as people do who do not yet know where they are going. The night was warm with spring, but Rose shrugged her coat round her neck. Large and placid, Mirek still walked apart.

On the embankment of the river street-lamps shone through the branches of trees, and along the twigs leaf-buds were beginning to show like knots. They stopped walking. He stood, a tall shadow in a dirty raincoat, and gave off melancholy in waves. How sad that the race should still produce people like him, when what was needed was someone more compact, as it were more resilient to atmospheric pressure.

'Let's look at the river.'

It flowed in a gulf in front of them, black and greasy.

Unhindered by buildings the wind brought a wild stench, like a blow on the face. It caught at their throats, roughened by the wine they had drunk in the Students' Club. The girl bent her head and choked. He came towards her.

'God, what is that?'

'It is from the cellulose factory outside the town. By night you can smell it a long way.'

She hurried across the bridge and he followed with long strides.

'It's terrible. How can people live here?'

'They are accustomed. I think it is much worse in the factory but that is one of the problems of reconstruction.'

'What do you mean?'

'It affects their brains and they become mad. This is an important industry and we make cellulose very cheaply. We cannot afford safety devices. And you see in this country people work where they are told. The workers are in power. They cannot strike against themselves, can they? That would be ridiculous.'

He spoke with polite ferocity, as though making a quick winning move in some competitive game.

'Has this been going on long?'

'Some years. But you see the river is quite poisoned.'

'Polluted. It's awful.'

The dead stream would always be flowing through Biala Gora. Rose knew the obsession which Mirek was trying to make her share: that nothing would ever go right here whatever they said, for hundreds of years.

'I don't believe it.'

'What?'

'About the factory.'

'It is what people say. I do not take visitors over this factory so I cannot know.'

'Can nobody find out for certain?'

'If they did? We may not write it in a newspaper. If it is not written about, how can people feel anything about it? With a censorship like ours we are not permitted a sense of injustice.'

'Someone must know the truth.'

'Why? Truth is for Western journalists and they do very well without it. We don't want it. We want fantasies.'

They arrived at the housing estate on the edge of the town, and the cinderpath leading to the Rudowskis' flat.

She turned towards him with a helpless gesture.

'Don't worry. You do not have to stay here. And perhaps we have got used to it.'

'Will it ever stop?'

'Nothing ever stops.'

'Damn.' She was wrestling ineffectively with the key, which fitted badly into the lock. She wanted him to go away; in spite of his healthy appearance, he was ill with unhappiness.

'Let me help.'

The lock yielded to him in one turn. He was very strong, breathing heavily there beside her in the dark. He put one hand on the corner of her shoulder.

'No,' she said. 'Sorry. Good night.'

Fifteen

IN the club, Derek Loasby was still dancing with Wanda.
He pulled his arm tightly round her and looked down at
her round head, which she had just had cropped short like
a boy's.

She and some of her friends had copied this hairstyle
from an American actress in a French film. This morning at
his Polish lesson, Miss Barcik had told him it reminded her
of the Camps: this new generation, she wailed, was repudi-
ating absolutely everything about their parents, the suffer-
ing as much as the ideals. Derek thought about this for a
little without agreeing and without being able to make up
his mind. Then he wondered where Miss Barcik had seen
him and Wanda together. It was not important but it gave
him the feeling of being watched.

He himself rather disliked Wanda's hair. It increased her
disconcerting air of detachment, and so did her sudden
blank stares and the little yawns she gave, as unrepented
as a cat's. True he had possessed her (on a Sunday afternoon
in the Students' Hostel, her room-mates being at the
cinema) but she still seemed only to possess herself.

Suddenly he noticed that Rose and Mirek had gone.

Derek felt deserted. All at once he was sure that he had
greatly overestimated the charm and interest of the young
people who surrounded him. You had to take their good
will on trust, for all the time there were muffled giggles

comments you didn't quite catch, and the sense that their very enthusiasm was isolating you. He held tightly on to Wanda while once again they circled the floor in and out of the stone pillars and past the squealing jazz group. He tried to think about tonight.

On his arrival at Biala Gora, he had been given a room at the Students' Hostel. After two weeks of discomfort and good intentions, he had deserted it. Now he lodged with a lawyer, his wife, their daughters and a cousin or two: the Tulewicz family had contracted, like a crab fitting all its legs into a rock-cleft, in order to make room for Mr. Derek Loasby, and he was never sure how many of them slept in the room next to his. Whenever he entered it, it was perfectly tidy, with heavily-fringed table cloths and potted plants and the usual row of divans round the walls.

Tonight he knew the flat would be empty and the stack of skis gone from the hallway, for the Tulewiczes were away in the mountains for the last of the snow. But while he was shepherding Wanda through the door he felt a qualm. It was like a blasphemy, this rape of the Catholic family atmosphere. And supposing one of the cousins should choose to return earlier? It would not seriously matter for himself but for Wanda it might.

In his room he switched on the bedside lamp. They undressed in the shadows. He lowered himself beside her, aching for the warmth of their complete embrace. Smiling he ran his hand over the blunt, cropped head. It was jerked away. Wanda burst into tears.

'What is it?'

He really wished to know, though he hoped the reason was flattering to himself.

He held her in his arms and her whole body was tense and shaking. She went on crying and he felt himself begin-

ning to get quite wet. Then she began to whisper to him —
all those repeated 'cz's' and 'sz's' reverberating in his ear,
like the inside of a sea-shell. When she stopped he had
understood nothing much, except that she had said he
would not understand.

Derek was in despair. He wanted above all to comfort
her, but the only obvious way seemed uncouth and insensi-
tive. Sometimes he wished it had all begun like that,
coarsely, paying her off each time with a pair of nylon
stockings. With Wanda, he was afraid this might have
worked.

He shifted the lampshade so that the light fell across her
body. She was staring past him with empty eyes; for her, he
was not there. The building was silent around them. There
was no sound from outside except for the lonely howl of
an east-bound train being driven towards the steppes.

'Why did you weep?'

She did not reply. He began to touch her again but she
held his hands away.

'It wouldn't be any good now,' he said, looking down his
stomach. He lit a cigarette and offered it to her, but she
refused it. She leaned over and pulled up the sheet.

'I will have to stay here till morning,' she said, bleakly.
'Because of the concierge.'

'The Tulewiczes are coming back in the morning.'

She fell asleep. He embraced her and held her, managing
to salvage something out of this defeat, and she did not
wake.

Later he watched the dawn whitening the opposite wall.
He was calmer now, but the bed was too narrow for them
both to sleep. His thoughts wandered off. On the wall there
hung pictures, nineteenth-century landscapes the Tulewiczes had brought from Wilno with the rest of their

furniture, after the German invasion of Russia. How had they managed it? You thought of the war here as being all massacre and chaos, yet there had been areas of normality, more then than afterwards, and to hear of them could still surprise you. All the same Derek, watching for the onset of morning, felt a muddled antagonism at the fact that the Tulewiczes had moved their furniture. His was a reaction fairly usual among foreigners; if anything at all went right here, you accused the inhabitants of being far better off than they said they were.

Derek's thoughts went back again and again to the girls he had danced with the previous evening, and how they spoke about him among themselves. Wherever he went, he walked into sudden silences, phrases were bitten back or breathed off in whispers he could not possibly understand. Sometimes he was almost proud of this, the free man in the Communist world, like a Sheriff striding the empty street at high noon with everyone watching him, but after such fantasies he quailed because he knew, compared with Mirek even, he was not free at all. He lived only on the information provided him, and if something was inexplicable like Wanda's tears he was utterly lost.

He fell asleep and when he awoke it was bright sunshine and after eight o'clock. Wanda was still beside him, awake and affectionate. But he was unmanned with apprehension, for the Tulewiczes would be returning at any minute. He got her out of bed but she took a particularly long time to dress, while he sat on the bed and bit his nails. After that she disappeared to the bathroom for about half an hour. Derek heard every banged door and scamper of feet announce the return of the Tulewicz children.

Finally she was gone. He stretched out, exhausted, and slept till noon.

Sixteen

JANET made a startled movement as if to protect some papers which were lying on the table in front of her.

'What are those?'

'The forms.'

'What forms?'

'For Tadeusz. For his passport.'

'Oh.'

Rose sat down opposite Janet and took one of her Bulgarian cigarettes. The sight of the papers, a step taken, disturbed her. Of course, Witek's promise had been given. Perhaps it was a mistake to have wheedled it out of him, to have bitched him into giving it, as she had done, for since then the poor man had gone round with a countenance of fixed glumness and an unkempt look. Still, a promise was a promise.

In Janet's elation there was something even more wrong. She kept on singing those wartime dance-tunes and reminiscing about her experiences at military hospitals with staff nurses, army doctors and even a 'very nice Canadian major who wanted to marry me, only he was killed at Dieppe. Rose had never heard of this character before; he was a ghost summoned up to dance at the defeat of Witold Rudowski.

In one way Rose understood her sister better now than she had previously done. Since talking to Mirek Sypniewski she was prey to the same sense of anguish about Tadeusz. His fate was in the air in a quite especial way; they all seemed to carry it around here, their past and their future, like an aureole or a spotlight following them, but Tadeusz alone might be given the right to choose.

'There's tea in the kitchen.'

When Rose came back with a glass of tea, she said: 'We oughtn't to push this too much, ought we? Not if it's going to mean a fuss.'

'If it's going to mean a fuss, that can't be helped. He has to sign.'

'He'll have to have photographs too, won't he? I mean, I don't see all this business about not telling him. It's treating him like a child and after all he is fifteen. I know we were treated like that but nowadays in England —'

'I mean Witek has to sign.'

'Oh, I see. Well, he promised.'

'I bet you he tries to wriggle out of it.'

If he does, Rose thought, it is your fault. She said: 'We'll have to persuade him again.'

'You persuade him. Your idea in the first place.'

'All right. But we could put it off, couldn't we?'

'No, we couldn't. He promised, you told me he promised. I won't have Tadeusz disappointed.'

'But Tadeusz doesn't even know about this.'

'He must go. I've set my heart on it. Don't you want him to go?'

'Yes, I do,' Rose said. 'For three weeks or so, anyway. Poor little beast, he deserves a good time.'

'I want him to learn what it is like to be English. Then he can choose. That's what the solicitors suggested, isn't it?'

'I suppose it is. I don't think they'd any idea how silly it sounds.'

Janet sulked at this and no further discussion took place
until Witek returned from the University. He looked
strained and haggard. There was a piece of his hair that
would not stick down. He saw the papers lying on the
table and at once guessed what they were.

He sat down and said: 'Rose.'

She was torn with pity to look at him. 'Yes.'

'I think perhaps this is not possible. So sorry.'

'I do not understand, Witek.'

He was trembling and on the other side of the table Janet
was trembling too. Rose loved them both, and was sorry for
them, and she dared not speak.

'Better not, this year,' Witek said.

'Rose has invited him. She has been kind enough —'

But he could not look at Janet. 'Rose?'

'I told you I wanted to and I thought you said "yes" but
if —'

He stood up and put his arm round her shoulders, lean-
ing on her, breathing close, touching her more heavily than
he had ever done before. One of his hands was tight on her
upper arm, the thumb pressing in where the muscle slipped
on the bone.

'Rose.'

'Yes?' She was frightened, feeling crushed against
him.

'May I speak with you alone, please?'

Rose looked despairingly at Janet, who turned away.

When they had gone, Janet unfolded the papers again
put on her spectacles and began to fill in the blank
spaces.

Rudowski, Tadeusz, born Glasgow, Scotland, 19 January
1944. Father: Rudowski, Witold Wlodzimierz, born Kato
wice, 2 May 1916. Mother: Nicholson, Janet Elizabeth

born Barnham, Surrey, England, 3 August 1922. Social
Class: Working intelligentzia.

She completed the whole questionnaire three times and
then sat back and lit a cigarette. Her hands were shaking.
Twenty minutes had gone past.

She heard somebody stumble over the bicycles in the
corridor. It was Rose, returning alone.

'Well?'

'Damn that bicycle. Yes, all right.'

Janet was silent and Rose saw that she had been crying.

Rose put her arm round her sister. 'Cheer up, it's all
right, I tell you.' But by now she herself felt badly in need
of convincing and so, as she usually did, she went on talking. 'Poor Witek, can you believe what he thought I was
up to? He thought I was going to kidnap Tadeusz and take
him to England and never let him come back. Honestly. I
mean, I suppose everyone suspects everyone here, but really
that does seem a bit much.'

Rose was talking against a gulf of anxiety. Things were
far worse than she had imagined and she was deeply sorry
for him.

'What did you tell him?'

'Oh, I gave him absolutely every guarantee under the
sun. Return ticket, to begin with. I said we'd only ask for a
six weeks' visa and I swore I'd see he got back when it was
finished. There was a bit of trouble because we couldn't
find anything I thought sacred enough to swear by. To
Witek I'm really a terrible pagan, aren't I? I mean, he's
always believed in something, hasn't he? But in the end
we made it. I told him I'm sure Tadeusz will be longing to get back. After all, he's a tremendous patriot, isn't
he?'

Janet did not speak.

'Actually I'm scared Tadeusz will be disappointed with England.'

'He's too young to be disappointed, except in people. He'll be thrilled.'

'I wonder. Well, there we are.'

'Thank you, darling.' At last Janet smiled.

'Anything to oblige. Now I've got to break the dreadful news to Tadeusz. Witek said I could.'

Seventeen

THE tram crossed a bridge over the polluted river and ran far out along the edge of the pine forest. At the last stop Tadeusz helped Rose to get down. They watched the tram grind round in a large circle and set off back to Biala Gora. Beside them a sandy track led away into the forest.

'Don't go out of sight. If you disappear I'll never find the way back.'

The boy did not react; he thought she was trying to make him feel important. Although this walk was one which they had promised each other since Rose's first day at Biala Gora, he did not appear to be particularly cheerful about it. There was a mulish look about him. He picked up a stick and began slashing away at things.

The forest was composed of pine trees. Paths and firebreaks ran through it, and occasionally there were black bubbling pools, round which the new sedge sprouted a brilliant green. From one of these came a riotous sound, honking and cackling.

'What on earth's that?'

'Frogs.' He threw his stick and the cackling stopped.

'You've frightened them. It was a lovely noise. They don't do that in England.' She walked towards the pool but the ground was marshy and she soon returned.

'In autumn we are coming here for mushrooms.'

99

'It's lovely. Thank you for bringing me. Look, there's a lizard. If you don't move they can't see you.'

Tadeusz immediately moved and the lizard ran away.

Rose watched him for a moment, surprised and a little put out by this lack of sympathy. He did not look at her. He picked up another stick and went on slashing the green plants.

'I'm sorry. Aren't you enjoying this?'

He did not answer for a moment. Then he said: 'I think English persons like going for walks.'

'Yes. Don't you?'

'Not just walks. We like to go to see something or to do something.'

'We've seen a lizard.'

He did not reply and they went on walking down one of the wide fire-breaks.

Suddenly he said: 'Mother says you have invited me to England.'

'Yes.' Rose drooped a little with disappointment. 'I did think she was going to let me break the dreadful news. Why didn't you tell me you knew? Oh, Tadeusz, you are pleased, aren't you?'

'Of course,' he said politely.

After a while he said: 'I want very much to go to England.'

'Then what the hell's wrong?'

When he sulked, he looked like his mother. He had retreated into one of those difficult corners where one holds out, at all costs, against showing gratitude.

Though they had been walking for only twenty minutes, they were now deep into the forest. There seemed no point in being where they were. Pinewoods are too dry and aseptic to be attractive in any way. They had nothing to do but talk to each other, but this was proving increasingly difficult. Rose was asking too much of him, trying to force out understanding and love. But there seemed to be nothing between them now, only this haze of polite English — it was Witek's English really, not Janet's at all — through which Tadeusz spoke to her.

'I know I shall think of Poland all of the time. Comparing things and — and arguing with myself. But it is not to be helped.'

'Try not to worry too much. You're young.'

'But I must learn about this.'

'There's nothing much you can do about it, is there?'

For Tadeusz this remark was worse than nothing. Of course you had to tackle everything while you still believed you could. Rose knew this but she was still annoyed and offended with him. She had made what was really an offer of love and he was too young for it. He had no idea yet that his indifference had any power to hurt.

'In any case,' he said gloomily, 'there is still the visa. Perhaps I cannot get it.'

'I'm going to Warsaw the day after tomorrow. I'll get the forms from the Embassy.'

'Going to Warsaw — then you are leaving?'

He was worried now, she noticed with a little stab of happiness. 'No, I'm coming back. I'm going to Krakow for a few days to stay with Mrs. Kazi — Kazi — thing's sister.'

Tadeusz thought about this. 'Krakow is a beautiful place. I was there with an excursion.'

'Yes, I'm sure it is.' She did not want to be put off now. 'I'll post the visa forms and you can have them ready before I come back.'

'I must have people to sign.'

'You can do that, too.'

'Even then perhaps I will not get the visa.'

'It oughtn't to be difficult. You're a student.'

'There is one girl I know that was refused.'

'Oh?'

'She was an orphan. They don't want orphans.'

'Well, you're not an orphan.'

He appeared not to be listening, but went on in a wondering voice: 'It is strange about England, they take in niggers but not Poles.'

She was appalled by this and wondered where he had learned it. 'You mustn't talk like that.'

'Why not?'

'Because — because people — my friends — won't like you. They'll think you are uneducated.'

This sounded inadequate but she thought it would do for him. He accepted it without comment. The essential thing was not to blame him, to go on talking as though nothing had happened; for the first time, however, she realized something of Janet's urgency to get him away from all this. He was damaged, but in a way that was unexpected; with his intelligence he could catch you off your guard.

Rose went on talking. She chattered to him about London, describing her flat where, now that her girl-friend had moved out, Tadeusz would be able to have a bedroom to himself for the first time in his life. She told him about the places they would visit together and the people she wanted him to meet.

Tadeusz walked quietly and intently, his face inexpressive. Rose could not tell if he was listening or not. The forest began to get thinner around them and now they were following a sort of sandy ravine which led on to a main road.

Tadeusz stopped.

'Tired already?'

He did not answer. His silence was heavy, meaningful.

Beside the track stood a large block of concrete with a plaque made of bronze let into the front of it. On the plaque there was a date, some writing in Polish, then the hoops and gallows of a Hebrew inscription.

'What's that?'

But she knew at once what it was. Two bunches of colts-foot lay on top of the block; a bumble bee tussled at one of the yellow flowers.

All afternoon the boy had been leading Rose through the pinewoods towards this place. For this reason he had suggested the walk, had taken the tram, and to counteract her natural cheerfulness had slashed sullenly at the vegetation and listened unmoved to all her chatter about London. This, with an intensity of adolescence almost like malice, he had been planning for her. Now he watched her. He wanted to know whether he had succeeded or not.

He translated the plaque. 'There were fifty-eight shot here. The others in Biala Gora were taken to the Camps.'

He was out of breath and his cheeks were flushed. He had failed absolutely, for Rose was only trying to imagine what it was like being Tadeusz.

Her second thought was that he could not possibly under-stand this himself or feel anything genuine about the skeletons in the sandy soil. It had happened in the year he was born, and he had been born in Scotland. 'This is what the Germans did here.' Yes, it was true but he had been told to say it. You shouldn't have to make propaganda, even true propaganda, to near relatives. They had damaged him, all right, even when they made him tell the truth. He was cor-rupted by the truth and this was what in the future it would be almost impossible to explain to him.

She gave him a look of deep pity and love. Now he, too, knew he had failed. He had meant her to assent and be in some way broken, but she only sympathized.

A few yards further on they emerged to the main road, which was lined with poplar trees.

'So this walk wasn't just a walk, after all.'

Tadeusz laughed. 'A Polish walk. Not an English one.'

He was relieved to have got his task over. He had given up sulking and was as confident and attractive as he had ever been.

Where the forest ended, huge fields stretched out, divided into a mosaic of little strips. Some women were thrusting seed potatoes into the thin soil.

'Tadeusz, do let's stop trying to prove things to each other. Come to England just for a holiday. No one's going to make anyone believe anything by pushing it down the other's throats.'

She was the one who failed now; he merely waved her away. He talked without stopping all the way back in the tram and they arrived home cheerful, confident and hungry, and friends for the first time.

Eighteen

TADEUSZ and Rose were walking down a long slope of grass towards the water. He had changed his mind now and was quite used to coming for walks for the mere pleasure of a beautiful day. Behind them somewhere Janet and Witek were following. Some sort of break-through had taken place; everything was going all right with them and from now on it always would. They were perfectly happy, as happy as one was in the summers of childhood. Boats were gliding up and down the lake — of course, it was the Serpentine! — and between the trees you could see the flash of the new glass buildings of Knightsbridge. To the right, though, over beyond the Barracks, stood a tall chimney which Rose did not remember having seen before. She had heard they were knocking down the Imperial Institute and this must be some part of the reconstruction plan. All the same, the black chimney looked out of place in the sky over South Kensington.

'That's the Imperial Institute, isn't it?' she asked Mirek Sypniewski.

He flinched at the word 'Imperial'.

'No, it's a factory,' he said.

'But it doesn't smell.'

'Nothing smells in dreams.'

Witek was gently shaking her shoulder. 'Five o'clock.'

She gasped with anguish, unable to remember where she was. The room was dark and Janet still slept.

Rose sat on the edge of the bed shivering. It was her first experience of the great Iron Curtain dream which, under the fences and naked sand of the frontiers, links up a world of sleepers with its vision of the summers which have for long been left out of the calendar.

In the kitchen Rose and Witek drank tea and chewed at pieces of bread. Tadeusz's bed was beside them; he lay in an almost frighteningly deep sleep, twisted as though he had been thrown down from a great height.

They took a workers' tram to the railway station. She had wanted to travel by air but Witek paid only half-fare on the trains. Witek had insisted on accompanying her, in order to surround her with attention: he felt that if she could see how smoothly it was possible to manage things, she would approve more both of the country and himself.

When they arrived at the station the platforms were almost empty, brightly lit and raked by a cold wind. The waiting-room however was crowded with people, soldiers, peasant women with bursting bundles, old men in suits of dark corduroy, children and young girls, who seemed to have been there all night at least, waiting for the train. There was nowhere else to go and nothing Witek could do to alleviate the impact which he imagined this must be having on Rose; but if he could have arranged the train an hour earlier, or hurried the sun into the sky, he would have done so.

When finally the train was shunted in, he was among the first to stampede the still-moving carriages. He secured a corner seat for her but in the ensuing struggle was forced out of his own place by a woman with a baby. Rose was left isolated, speechless, while Witek retreated to the corridor. Their journey was to take five hours.

The train did not move off for another hour.

The lamps paled along the platform, where soldiers and militiamen were pacing up and down to keep warm. There was no real dawn; everything became dully visible, the darkness going away like a strain from the eyes. The train shuddered and began to move. Factories slid away; there was a long view of fields, and from time to time a river, a battered village or an old woman watching a cow.

Witek threw anxious looks in Rose's direction. He was ashamed of the rough appearance of the peasants in the carriage. He had no sense of common identity with them but only of impatience that they existed, in such large numbers and so obviously not up to standard. After about twenty minutes he leaned across to ask Rose if she was comfortable.

She was not, but nothing was to be gained by saying so.

Now that her suspected foreignness was confirmed, the other passengers reacted to it in different ways. Two or three turned their heads away and did not look at her for the remainder of the journey. The woman next to her, however, gave a little fluttering smile. Rose made gestures of admiration at the baby; it was a sturdy child with a large nose and a positive attitude.

The train moved slowly across a plain which seemed designed for a battlefield and had often been exactly this. The landscape was uninteresting but there were always people in sight, for all grazing animals must be watched and discouraged from wandering. Goose girls drove their flocks over the shorn grass and little boys threw stones at horses to keep them off the railway line.

A boy came swaying down the corridor expertly carrying a tray with glasses of boiling tea. Most of the passengers took one. Rose burnt her hands. The woman next to her blew on the tea for a moment, then gave a sip of it to the baby. The baby fixed Rose with a solemn and perplexed stare, and was suddenly very sick.

Rose at once put her tea on the floor, stood up and took a box of English Kleenex from her night-case. Together, she and the woman cleaned up the baby and threw the balls of soiled paper out of the window. Rose gave the rest of the Kleenex to the woman. The blue and white box excited comment and admiration and was handed all round the compartment. After this, she decided to give up her seat so that the baby, which was far too large for the woman's lap, could lie down and sleep.

She joined Witek in the corridor. He gazed at her with affection, he was delighted to be travelling with her, but, because the peasants were disappointing and the baby had been sick (though very obviously it had been a well-fed baby) he felt he had to keep apologizing.

Rose managed to quieten him down. She asked him what he was going to do in Warsaw. He produced a slip of paper on which he had planned out his day. Rose's time-table was consigned to the margin of this. At the centre was his appointment with Mrs. Goldberg at the Ministry of Higher Education: 'I am confident that she will have some good news today about our English philology department.' He would also be visiting the bureau of the State Publishing House which dealt with textbooks. 'They wish to reprint my book — with some important revisions, of course. And then —'

Rose interrupted him. 'What about Tadeusz's passport? You said you'd do something about that.'

'Yes. I have an acquaintance at the Foreign Ministry. I shall telephone.'

'Good.'

Somewhat ruffled, he went back to his list, from which this item had been omitted. Rose would be visiting her friends Mr. and Mrs. Tatham. Was the pronunciation correct? He would not call for her there but would look for her, during the afternoon, at the British Institute. 'You will have an opportunity to meet with Mr. Pilkington. He has been very helpful to me.' From there they would go to take a small cup of coffee, prior to Rose's departure on the afternoon plane.

'You will be staying long in Krakow?' he asked her.

This had been discussed several times in his presence. But Janet and he each possessed the faculty of becoming deaf when the other was addressed.

'Four days.'

'And then?'

'Back to Biala Gora.'

'I wonder if you will be pleased with Krakow.'

'They say it is very beautiful.'

'I wonder if you will be pleased with the people.'

'Why?'

'Other Polish people do not like them. They say they did not have the war there. Only one house was bombed.'

'You mean the other people wanted it all to be bombed?'

'They say Krakow people did not suffer so much.'

'Then they only like people when they have suffered?'

It might be true. If you had not suffered, you had less reality for them and they could not concentrate on you for very long. Whenever she was with Witek, she felt he liked her as a person but also considered her as a symbol of something which was not very praiseworthy; like the inhabitants of Krakow, she was classified, dismissed.

You could not judge him harshly, however, when you considered what he had to put up with in the normal run of events. He was returning to Biala Gora tonight, by the train which arrived at four in the morning. He had early classes tomorrow. This was the sort of procedure he was used to, travelling underfed on dawdling trains, waiting in anterooms, suing for power and action at the Ministry. Only with so few other pleasures available, it was perhaps easier for him to sacrifice himself to useful ambition.

Nineteen

'OH, Rose, you must tell us what it was like, was it simply ghastly, we're longing to know. What are you going to drink, I expect you need one, I know I do. Mark will be back fairly soon. You don't mind the children coming in for a bit, do you? They've just been on one of Nanny's smashing walks and I always feel they need reindoctrinating a bit after that, don't you know. Nanny's such a fearful fascist reactionary, it simply isn't true.'

During the ten days since Rose had seen her, Alexandra gave the impression of having increased in bulk and resplendency. In black stockings and a scarlet wool dress designed to celebrate rather than camouflage her pregnancy, she stood wide-legged with her behind to a blazing fire. Her fair skin, her shining teeth and eyes were almost cruelly healthy after the deadened complexions and steel-rimmed mouths of Biala Gora.

Rose drank whisky and retreated into the depths of her armchair. Alexandra did not ask her any more questions. Three small children in gaiters were shepherded in by the nanny. For a few minutes the room was full of their shrill voices in counterpoint to a complicated story which the nanny was telling; a toy had been left behind on the grass and an elderly lady — 'she was ever so heavily made up but her English was quite good' — had picked it up, brought it to them, and then wanted to buy it. 'Of course, it was

Simon's own tedda so I couldn't really offer to do anything to oblige her, could I? There'd have been ructions.'

To Rose watching, this scene was like a pastoral entertainment at a considerable move from reality. So Tadeusz and Mirek and such people must have observed her, and felt that the things she told them of London were played out on an apron stage with a set of conventions as remote and arbitrary as a court masque. Only the elderly lady in the nanny's story could be recognized: she gave one the feeling of where one was.

After lunch Mark offered to drive Rose to the British Institute.

'Don't bother yet, please. My brother-in-law won't be there till three-thirty.'

'Come on. I'll show you some of the city.'

She watched him as he drove, liking him more but still a little frightened of him. He was conventional and even pompous, but he was also really interested in what happened. His pompousness was mitigated by the fact that when some situation appeared comic (he did not like wit) he could be seen unexpectedly shaking and weeping with silent diaphragm-heaving giggles.

'This is Lazienki Park. Like to have a look?'

'All right.'

A group of people watched them get out of the foreign car with CD plates. Further down the path some children were feeding a red squirrel. It jerked to and fro like a clockwork toy, and scrambled all the way up a man's arm. It had thin fur and a degenerate-looking face.

The park stretched out in limpid sunlight, with some of the trees still showing the amputations of shell fire. Ornamental water wandered in and out, and there were swans. a rustic bridge, a Greek theatre. Yellow scaffolding crisscrossed the little Lazienki palace, which was then being restored. The whole place was beautiful but had a strange, vaguely unhappy look, as though it were being called back unwillingly from the past; Rose thought suddenly of those two English ladies at Versailles.

In the middle of the park they sat down on a bench.

'How is your sister? Really, I mean.'

She glanced at Mark, unwilling to offer evidence of unhappiness to anybody so detached and so successful. He was gazing across the water at the Greek Theatre. He sat with his long legs crossed, the right foot twisted back under the left ankle. She had never liked men who were able to do this or who kept their handkerchiefs up their sleeve. His sister Elizabeth, however, had always told her that Mark was good, using the word with an odd precision, like a technical term.

'Is she happy?'

'No, not at all.'

'I see.'

'Mark, it's been awful —' and now she had started, she told him all about Janet and Witek and their competition over Tadeusz.

'Poor Rose.'

'I'm the last to be pitied. I feel after this none of us, you, me, anyone in England, ought to pity ourselves ever again.'

He was silent at this, and threw away his cigarette.

'I was afraid it might be like that. I didn't tell you this, until you'd seen for yourself. I've met your sister.'

'No? When? She didn't tell me.'

'No, I suppose not. She turned up at the Embassy. I happened to be around, I can't remember how it was now. She was pushed on to me. The Consul usually looks after these things.'

'When was this?'

'Last autumn. Soon after I got here.'

'It was probably my fault then. You see, I wrote that you were being sent here. She met Elizabeth when she was in England.'

'Oh, so that was it.' He sounded irritated.

'What did she want?'

He gave a sort of incredulous snort. 'She asked if I could arrange for her to go to England.'

'Oh, God!' Rose was silenced by this for a moment. 'What did you say?'

'Your sister knew the position really. She has dual nationality. She can get a British passport whenever she wants. But if she did that I don't know that the Poles would let her come back. The real trouble always is the children. They are Poles and we can't help them.'

'Did she mention Tadeusz?'

'No, I don't think so.'

'Perhaps she thought he could be included in her passport.'

'She couldn't do that. He's Polish.'

'He was born in England. Scotland, actually. Glasgow.'

'They won't recognize that here, I'm afraid.'

'No. And last autumn, of course, nobody knew about my aunt's money.'

Mark said: 'When I explained to your sister about the passports, she went away and I thought perhaps she might have settled down again. On the whole it's the intelligent ones who've managed to stick it. The Scottish mill girls and people like that have all gone home.'

'I suppose so.' Rose wondered if Janet was intelligent.

'I thought I'd better tell you that she'd been to see us

before she knew anything about this money. Incidentally, who *does* know about it? '

' She does.'

' Nobody else? '

' My brother-in-law doesn't know. He is just getting a new job, and, of course, he's in with the Party.'

' You'll have to tell him sometime. It'll be a bit of a test for him: expediency or belief.'

' Oh, he believes in it all right. If you have anything to do with education, you might. But if you worked in a shoe factory you probably wouldn't.'

Mark laughed at this. ' So you can't tell him yet? '

' No. And so we can't tell Tadeusz.'

' What are you going to do, then? '

' I —' She stopped. At this moment she couldn't tell him about inviting Tadeusz to England. It would appear devious, and was not. Mark might be unconvinced of this, however, and she suspected he could arrange to stop the visa. Rose was learning suspicion easily.

' Oughtn't I to wait, Mark? I want to invest the money and the income and hold on. This can't go on for ever. Tadeusz'll be grown up and able to make up his own mind. Besides, things may get better.'

' Perhaps. Perhaps not. The other thing is they could apply for an emigration visa. Sometimes whole families get these.'

' No good, I'm afraid. Witek certainly doesn't want to leave, nor does Tadeusz.'

Mark laughed shortly. He stood up and then looked at his watch. These difficulties had made him lose interest. ' Then I suppose your idea is best. Waiting, I mean.'

' I suppose so. If only everyone *can* wait.'

They walked slowly up the hill to the car.

While he was unlocking the doors he said: 'By the way, it is better not to discuss these things in the car.'

This remark took away any easiness that was left from the Spring afternoon. They had sat and talked in the park only because there were no microphones there.

Later Mark tried to make some amends: 'I don't know how long your visa's for, but I do wish you'd come and stay with us for a few days. Alexandra would love to have you.'

'Thank you, Mark. The only thing is, while I've got time, I feel I should go back to my sister.'

'Of course.'

'But a day or two would be lovely.'

'Let us know, will you?' He stopped the car. 'This is the place. No, I'll come up, too. There's a book they were meant to be keeping for me.'

The stairway of the British Institute was lined with travel posters, Woburn Abbey, the Giants' Causeway, the Trooping of the Colour. In the reading-room some battered-looking old ladies, reading *Vogue* and the *Illustrated London News*, eyed the newcomers furtively: perhaps it was one of these who had offered to buy Simon Tatham's teddy bear. There was no sign of Witek Rudowski.

In the Library Rose and Mark were confronted by a small scarlet-faced man. He was dressed in violently checked tweeds of a type usually only worn by peers or bookies, and then only in the immediate proximity of a horse.

'Hullo, hullo, Mark old boy, how very nice to see you! How is Alexandra? And the children? Alexandra's ragtime band! Ha! ha! I won't forget that in a hurry.'

Mark did not flinch.

'Rose, this is George Pilkington. Rose Nicholson.'

Mr. Pilkington eyed Rose, found her pretty and hurriedly

looked away. 'Over here on a visit? Weather's turned out well for you, hasn't it? Looks like we'll be getting a game of tennis again, Mark, before we know where we are.'

After the quietness, the grey subdued confidences on the verge of despair to which Rose had been subjected in the last few days, this man's voice, like Alexandra's, was strangely discomfiting.

She moved away as soon as she conveniently could, while the two men went on talking. With nothing better to do she took a book from the shelves at random: it was a large expensive-looking volume on soil erosion. The date of cataloguing was June 1946, the year of publication, a year in which soil conservation still provided another of the fairly easy answers. Here in the British Institute this book had survived Mikolajczyk, Bierut, Stalin and Rokossowski. Rose turned back to the fly-leaf: it was virgin. Nobody had ever taken the book out of the library.

'See if we can't get our revenge on H.E. in this year's doubles, what?'

A timid secretary approached. 'Dr. Rudowski is here, Mr. Pilkington.'

As soon as the girl was out of earshot, Pilkington rolled his eyes and bit his lips with histrionic rage. 'These people, they're incredible! I ask you, this one seems to think I've got nothing better to do than sit around all day listening to his views on teaching English. I tell him again and again that's quite outside my scope, but does it make a ha'porth of difference? Oh dear me no. As far as I'm concerned, he's the biggest clot on this or any other side of the Iron Curtain.'

Rose pushed the book on soil erosion back into the shelf. 'Excuse me, I think he's looking for me.'

'Who is?'

'Dr. Rudowski.'

Pilkington stared at her with popping eyes. 'You don't know him, do you?'

'Yes. He's my brother-in-law.'

Beside them, Mark Tatham was shuddering convulsively. He was like an asthmatic, or someone stopped during the parturition of an overwhelming sneeze. His face darkened and tears of laughter broke from his eyes and trickled down his cheeks.

Twenty

'I AM sorry we could not have some conversation with Mr. Pilkington. He is a very interesting man.'

'Oh, Witek, no, he's terrible.'

He accepted it now as a good joke, her condemnation of everyone he recommended and he smiled warmly to show that he appreciated it. They were sitting in a café near the air terminal, where they had left Rose's suitcase. They had glasses of weak coffee in front of them.

'Perhaps you should not take so much coffee. It may make you nervous.'

Kind, weary and ponderous, a supporter of the Established Order, there was after all nothing in Witek which could appeal to the English. Rose held on to her right to defend him to the utmost; she tried to avoid thinking that, whatever happened to Aunt Louise's money, it was he who finally must be deceived and defeated.

'It's all right.' She was already trembling a little. '*Reisefiebez*, you know, before the aeroplane. Tell me, have you had a good day?'

'I have excellent news for you, excellent.'

'About Tadeusz's passport? Is it going to be all right?'

He stopped, checked in his course. 'No, not that. That is — we must wait.'

'Oh, I see. Well, go on.'

'It is about our department of English Philology. We are

to have examinations this summer and twelve students are to be admitted.'

'Witek, that's wonderful. And you'll be in charge.'

'Unfortunately, not yet. At the moment we are obliged to have Professor Mikulski, the professor of Russian, to supervise. But he is a good man and very conscientious. And I will set the entrance examinations.'

'I see.' She wondered if this professor was a good man in the way Elizabeth had said Mark Tatham was, and what it meant.

'I'm very happy for you, Witek.'

'And now I must work on my thesis for becoming Docent. Without this I cannot be Head of our department. I am afraid, even before that, they may choose another man.'

'But can they do that now?'

'Unfortunately yes. There is one of the lecturers of Warsaw University. Some persons think he is a good scholar but I do not think his methods are modern ones. His thesis was "The Versification of Sir Gawain and the Green Knight".'

Rose fidgeted with her coffee glass. 'I realize now I've met him.'

'Yes?'

'On my first day here. He was at lunch.'

Witek could not resist the temptation to hear Rose, in her brusque way, condemn somebody else.

'Did you think well of him?'

'Yes. He's very nice and intelligent.' She saw his disappointment and added: 'Of course he's a fearful reactionary.'

Her hand jerked nervously and coffee spilt in the saucer. She was furious with herself, not so much for betraying Adam Karpinski, whom she scarcely knew, but for reducing everything to the level of Alexandra and Nanny: for not taking seriously lives which were fought out in an atmosphere of risk and apprehension.

Since her conversation with Mark Tatham in Lazienki Park, this atmosphere was a sick feeling in the air; everything, sky, street and buildings had grown a little darker. Once you began to think about it, suspicion was everywhere. Did Witek know of Janet's visit to the British Embassy last autumn? Did he think Rose's appearance here this spring was something to do with that, and not entirely to the pleasures his country offered? Everyone here had secrets, the truths you could utter at any moment and must keep simmering in your head behind your tongue. In this atmosphere a betrayal must be like a move towards liberation, the relief from a whispering insistent pressure.

Only Witek was out of this, worrying about his own career. 'And that man is Docent, from Warsaw University. He had many friends among the older professors.'

'But you have friends, too, surely.'

'Not so many. Mrs. Goldberg at our ministry. Dr. Zwiersz in our University Council, Professor Mikulski, one or two more. They understand that it is important, what we want to do.'

'I see.'

'The old methods are no longer suiting the students of the new generation. We cannot have professors who are interested only in one or two students who can become scholars or assistants. Everyone has to work, everybody must be useful.'

'Of course. It's obvious, isn't it?' She looked at her watch; there were another ten minutes until the bus left.

'To them, not.'

'But, Witek, it's you who are starting the department. You'll be able to show them what to do.'

E

'You are very kind to me, Rose.' He shifted his chair a little nearer; once again there was the problem of his breath. 'Rose, I know I am not the best, I know my English is not perfect but I learn only late in life, in England. When I married I spoke only a little — you can still remember?' Rose nodded. He was enjoying humiliating himself rather too much.

'I was frightened of your mother. She was the sort of lady who never realized that some others could not speak English.'

'Oh, Witek, you shouldn't have worried. She never listened to what other people said. It made no difference.'

He smiled. 'Yes, I think sometimes after I married she wondered who I was. She had been told but she was not listening.'

'She was glad you were a Catholic, though.'

Witek went into a sort of mumbling silence.

'I'm sorry — I didn't mean —'

'No, the Catholic church has done much good for our country in the past.'

'Probably. I couldn't take the Convent though — that was my trouble.' She looked at her watch again. 'We must go, mustn't we?'

They stood together in front of the airport bus.

'Witek, I *am* pleased, really. I mean, everybody in authority thinks you are absolutely all right. So there's no need for you to worry about Tadeusz going to England any more, is there?'

'No — yes.' He smiled. 'Please, though, remember that I want him back.'

As she kissed him, she said in a childish voice: 'Of course. How many more times do I have to promise?'

Witek watched her get on to the bus with a pang of loss.

He would miss her. It was true that she did not know what all this meant to him, but she was the only one who knew at what cost, against what an emptiness and absence of private affections, he had attained this point in his career. Standing outside the bus in the warm spring evening, he offered his success to Rose, with love.

Twenty-one

FROM the window of Adam Karpinski's flat, in a new block near the intersection of two avenues, Marszalkowska and Jerosolimskie, you look down on to the Polonia Hotel. This is practically the only substantial building to survive the destruction of the city, and now its ugly elaborate façade is like a face which appears in a dream in a wrong country and a wrong era. Adam could remember staying there in 1938, while visiting the capital with his parents. The city he had seen with the sharp eyes of a fourteen year old possessed a sort of Platonic reality for him: it subsisted somewhere else and even today, in certain dream states induced by vodka or love or tiredness, the grey Stalin-period buildings would dissolve like so many screens and that *Ur*-city reassemble its fragments, the Ghetto and the Royal Palace arise from nothing again and even the main railway station, where the family arrived and departed for the country, would manage to disinter itself from under the colossal weight of the Palace of Culture.

This afternoon, however, the sun shone and everything was real. Shelves of books, in various languages, still gathered the dust which the new building exhaled from its brittle plaster. There was no room for pictures and the few he possessed Adam had let his divorced wife take with her. They had waited years on a list for this new flat; he was glad to leave the old one, which had witnessed terrible

124

events, but he had left his wife behind on the way. Because he was a writer he was permitted two rooms, one to work in. He had no need of taste — there was nothing much to have taste about — and the apartment was a machine for his various activities and from the window he could watch the new Warsaw rise, which was something with which he was painfully involved.

He packed a suitcase, switched off the refrigerator, and locked the door. He left behind a chess-board, set out with a game in progress by telephone with one of his University colleagues (the friend was already defeated; Adam would win in three moves) and a bunch of red roses, ribbon and asparagus fern, presented by his seminar students on his birthday.

Adam walked down Marszalkowska towards the air terminal, past flowerstalls and wooden palings which were pasted with fresh witty posters for ancient Westerns. At one of the kiosks he brought an armful of literary weeklies, their yellow pages closely printed and stuffed out with the reviews and commentaries and bloc-notes of an always articulate intelligentzia. At least two contained articles by himself. He was the first to take a seat in the airport bus.

He watched Rose approach across the pavement with Witold Rudowski and swore gently. One of those mildly ridiculous swear-words: it meant 'dog's blood'. He had not at first recognized her; the context was so completely different from luncheon at the Tathams'. Then he remembered that the girl was in fact related to Rudowski. All the same, he protested that a peasant like that should be with a girl who, apart from being pretty and well-dressed, was also a friend of the Tathams.

One might accept Rudowski as a scientist or a politician; indeed, one accepted him or, rather, different versions of him, every day. But beside the late Professor Dybowski or beside the late Professor Stankiewicz, and all those high-domed philologists of the past generation — who had trained at German universities and, in several cases, afterwards died in German camps — Rudowski was a figure of farce, a mere puppet dangling on the strings of a few bargain-basement ideas. On closer inspection, even this English girl Rose, this English Rose, appeared to be addressing him with a patronizing air.

Rose climbed in and sat near the front of the bus. She waved through the door at Rudowski, and his decent peasant face beamed back at her. The bus began to move away.

Adam put his face near the window, so that he caught the full afterglow of Rudowski's farewell to Rose. The eyes of the two men stabbed at each other through the glass. Rudowski flinched. His smile disintegrated into abject worry. Adam grinned fiendishly.

The bus gathered speed, carrying Adam and Rose off together. He settled back in his seat and went on watching Rose. There was a new warmth in having her there, about five yards distant, while worried Rudowski stumped off round Warsaw on his clumsy intrigues.

Rose had a bright clearness which was not really connected with any colour in her head or clothing. He was appreciating this, and the line of hair, cheek and arm, so that it came as a shock to perceive that, like Rudowski, she was undergoing a temporary illness of worry. Her shoulders shifted under its burden and her hand kept going to her face. Believing herself unobserved, she could allow herself to look desperate. As he watched, he became so much absorbed in this that he was quite unconscious of the rows of seats which lay between them. He was with her, hearing the inaudible noises of her distress, amused and at the same time liking her because she was not indifferent, as one had so often heard the English to be.

To the others in the bus she was a foreigner and therefore happy. But Adam was not so stupid as to believe material comforts made life less 'real' or their possessors insensible to emotion. Still, she was young and smart, and anguish came more surprisingly from her.

He kept her in sight at the airport, following her across the tarmac to the little Ilyushin aeroplane. When the passengers stood in a group listening for their names to be called, he lost her, but there she was again in the aeroplane, only a few seats ahead of him, huddled against the window. When the stewardess stopped beside her with a tray of boiled sweets, Rose took one with a sort of blind, pawing movement.

The aeroplane taxied slowly across the field, swung round and stopped. Seagulls fleered up and resettled, further away. A few spots of water struck the thick glass of the windows.

'Miss Rose Nicholson. May I sit here, please?'

The surprise took her far more violently than he expected. She coloured fiercely, had a moment's difficulty with the sweet in her mouth, stammered something. Then the twin engines roared up. Outside, the seagulls, fields and low sheds began racing backwards.

It was quieter in the air and he heard her say: 'You shouldn't move while the plane is taking off.'

Used to jet planes, however, Rose herself had forgotten that this provincial veteran would be circling sharply. When it lurched sidewards she fell towards him. He felt her bones against him, she smelt as exotic as the Western world, while beyond her small face the wing-tip dropped like a stone, and below them stood the Palace of Culture, an axle with the whole grey city gyrating around it.

'I didn't hear your name called out,' she said.

'You remember my name?'

'Of course.'

The engines roared up. 'Someone else's ticket.'

'What?'

'Perhaps I'm using someone else's ticket.'

'In England you can't do that.'

He grinned. 'No, in England you can't do that.'

'What happens if we all get killed? Nobody will know who you are.'

He grinned. 'Nobody. It will be most confusing.'

She looked out of the window. Webs of cloud were floating past, and the flat country lay far below. On her other side, Adam Karpinski filled up the whole of the view.

'Do you mind if I smoke my pipe?'

'No, please do.'

When he produced it, however, Rose eyed it doubtfully, as though it was an assertion of Englishness she could not quite approve of.

'Have you seen anything of the Tathams?'

'I had lunch there today.'

He got the pipe going and said: 'I'm very fond of them both — Alexandra is a terrific girl.'

Rose noticed that certain expressions brought, like this one, a cawing note into his voice, as though he were mimicking the traditional conception of an English 'toff'.

'I don't know her well,' Rose said. 'She scares me a bit.'

'There used to be girls like that here, before the war. Now they are too expensive for our Socialist economy.'

'Well, Alexandra's got money of her own.'

'Are the Bermondseys rich?'

'I suppose they are.'

She resisted what might be a foreigner's clamorous interest in the English upper classes, and was silent.

He watched her for a little, then said: 'Why are you going to Krakow, if I may ask?'

'To see it.'

She hated having to explain herself, and in any case the whole operation seemed more and more of a mistake to her. She was not here to look at places, but to look after people. It was not her fault that the people, with the exception of Tadeusz, had proved so unsatisfactory.

'I was told I had to see Krakow.'

'Of course. We Poles are always informing foreigners that we have lost everything. But we must also show them what we have lost.' He pulled at his pipe. 'That is, if they are at all interested.'

'I *am* interested,' Rose said plaintively.

'Or very polite.'

'No. One gets tired of being polite.'

'Nobody can talk politely about what has happened to us.' Adam said.

'But it has happened everywhere, surely. Not just in Krakow.'

'It means more in Krakow. After all it was the old capital, it was one of the outposts of the West against barbarism and it held out against everyone from the Tartars onwards. And in 1848 it rebelled against three empires at once, can you imagine that? But in 1944 your two English-speaking empires handed us over to the barbarians. So it is a sad place now. You will see.'

'Why sadder than anywhere else?'

'You will see. Perhaps it was better that nothing was left

E*

of Warsaw. In Krakow you can still see the signs and relics and memorials of what we once were. Everywhere else it has all gone.'

'Surely not.'

'Yes, it has all gone. We are just survivors, by mistake. Our neighbours always wanted to destroy us and next time they will do it properly.'

As she had with Mirek Sypniewski, Rose found that this sort of conversation dragged one deep into the speaker's orbit. She could barely hear what Adam was saying, being deafened both by the engines and by the physical impact of his presence. She was afraid that it was his vehemence that gave him all his attraction and if he stopped addressing her he might somehow deflate and become another of the pudding-featured passengers who filled the rest of the seats of the aeroplane. But while he talked, he was wonderful. The Rudowskis were forgotten. She had left their world of domestic irritation and entered one of tragedy and glory.

The plane began to wheel and descend into the darker evening. They felt a jolt of warm air over the iron foundries of Nowa Huta.

There was a bus beside the hangar. Rose and Adam sat waiting for it to leave. He had given her his vision; he looked tired.

'You are staying at Francuski?'

'No, what is that?'

'The Hotel.'

'No. With friends.'

He speculated a little about this. 'Seeing how the poor live?'

'But why are they so poor in Krakow?' she asked. 'You said they had no war damage.'

'And they didn't have the money which rebuilt the

other towns. In any case, everybody is poor. Terribly poor. *You* cannot imagine.'

'I try. I've been staying with my sister.'

'They are rich. They both can work.'

'They seem poor to me.'

'To you, of course. You're Fanny—' he raised a placatory hand—'No, don't get worried, please. You—are—like—Fanny Price: "Though Mansfield Park might have some pains, Portsmouth could have no pleasures." Poland can have no pleasures.'

Though she already felt she knew him extremely well, she puzzled over this as she had over his pipe. *Mansfield Park* however was an aspect of his profession. Perhaps his knowledge of English slang also was.

'I'm not looking for pleasures. You think because you've all suffered so much here, other people are indifferent. But we do try to feel. At least I do. I must. And I think there are good things, as well as bad.'

'Wait till you have seen Krakow, seen how some of the old people live, people like Magda Wahorska, the Palewska girls and their mother, the old Princess. They had everything, remember, and they lost it all.'

She was happy and excited by the antagonism between them. But she did not react to the name of Mrs. Wahorska the sister of Mrs. Kazimierska. She was getting used to such conversations full of little gulps of silence, of things you preferred not to say.

Twenty-two

THE two women rose early and were out to Mass in the Old City. On their return Antosia, the maid, folded away the blankets from the pair of hard *chaises longues* they slept on, and went into the corridor to light the gas. Her mistress moved towards the door of the second room and put her ear to it, listening for the sounds of the girl sleeping. After a few moments she tapped and opened the door.

Rose had been awake for some time, had heard them go out and stayed wondering what to do and not wishing to be in the way. It was indeed difficult to move around, the rooms being so much cluttered with furniture that if you were to shift one object it would appear to blaze a trail of prying curiosity. So she stood still, looking out at the roofs and bell-towers of the city, and thinking about Adam and about Tadeusz.

At the sight of Rose, standing in the sunlight, wrapped in a silk dressing gown and brushing her hair, the two women made noises of admiration. Antosia hurried off to the kettle which was drumming and blowing in the corridor. She returned with tea and bread and butter.

'It is excellent tea,' Mrs. Wahorska said. 'We have already, I am afraid, been tasting a little.'

'But it is for you. Please do not waste it on me, I can have it any time.'

The old woman's eyebrows were raised at this and she

observed Rose without friendliness; evidently, she had not forgiven the awkwardness of the previous evening.

The difficulty had begun at the bus stop. Adam had said goodbye abruptly; it seemed he was certain of seeing her again, though she had no idea when or where this might be. She was alone and therefore herself unmistakable when the two shabbily-dressed females approached her. Remembering Kazimierska's great height Rose headed for Antosia, who was large and square, but a brisk angry little woman interposed herself. She was furious and there was to be no laughing it off. While they walked across the public gardens, one difference indeed became clear. The former Countess Wahorska had still a long young stride, like an English girl brought up in the country, while the servant took the waddling steps of the bundle-carrying peasant woman. But a greyness of poverty had taken away all other distinctions; Adam was right: this was worse than either Biala Gora or Warsaw.

Later, unpacking her suitcase. Rose said: 'I have brought you a present of tea.'

Her hostess examined the packet with suspicion. '*C'est du thé, ou du Lipton?*'

'*Thé*,' said Rose, who had been unaware of this distinction. '*Chinois*.'

'You do not take our tea? You wish to drink only this?'

'No, it is for you. I brought it from England.'

'I find that curious, since you did not then know that we should meet.'

This morning nothing had changed: Rose was meant to ask questions and do as she was told. Besides, Mrs. Wahorska spoke French, that domineering language, far better than she did.

'This room belongs to my daughter. Up to now, I am

allowed to keep it. But perhaps someone who does not like me will say something, and I shall have strangers put here.'

'Strangers?'

'Perhaps a whole family. One cannot know.'

'But won't your daughter come back?'

Antosia brought another glass and a saucer with rounds of lemon.

'Look, Antosia has found a lemon for us. She has a cousin at a State Grocer's Shop.' Rose's question remained to be answered. 'My daughter has been in Paris for three years. She intends to prolong her scholarship.'

'I see. What does she do?'

'Art history, naturally. My niece Halina who comes this afternoon, also. Halina works in the museum this morning and so you must put up with me. I have my lessons in the afternoon and evening. That photograph is of my son. It is not a good one but we never thought, in 1939, that there would be no opportunity of taking others.'

While she was talking a succession of bangs and clattering sounds echoed from the house beneath them.

'Those are the workmen.' The old woman suddenly acquired an air of extreme constraint and embarrassment. 'I regret I must tell you, they use our lavatory in the corridor, it is rather disagreeable. If you would prefer Antosia can bring —'

'No, of course not,' Rose said quickly. 'What are they doing?'

'They are transforming our house into a museum for the Workers' Party.' The first warmth came into the old lady's face. 'Imagine, my dear, this was my father's house. My great-grandfather built it. But, you know there is a point where one cannot complain any more but only laugh. So I had my friends'—a string of names followed,

including the ones Adam had mentioned the evening before — 'for my name-day and I made the announcement
that they are transforming the house into a Museum for
the Workers' Party and we all laugh. We cannot help it,
we cannot stop laughing. Staszek Kopczinski, he is my
nephew and a very brilliant man, said: "They put all our
things in museums and everybody goes to admire them, but
all they will have for their own place will be a few photographs and some old pamphlets which everyone laughs at
because they are in such bad Polish! "'

The old woman sat back and wiped weak sardonic tears
from her eyes.

'When you are ready we may go out. Later Antosia will
prepare dinner for us.'

'I want to invite you. I was told the hotel restaurant is
good.'

The other looked as if she were being offered charity,
which was unwelcome.

'Please come. If it's true about it being good, I mean.'

'That, I cannot tell you. For many years none of us
could afford it, and we did not like to be seen there with
foreigners. Now perhaps it does not matter for what more
can they do to us?'

After Rose had dressed, her hostess reappeared in a coat
and hat, both trimmed with fur which seemed not merely
old but to have come from sick animals in the first place.
However, heavily powdered and rouged as she was, the old
lady managed to look both fierce and spritely.

'Today we will use the grand staircase, where the men
are working.'

'Won't they mind?'

The old lady snorted.

They went through a doorway and down some stairs

which gave on to the mezzanine floor. The house dated from the late eighteenth century, and marble columns rose on each side of the grand staircase. Across the wall at the head of the stairs, there had already been set up a sepia 'photomural' of Lenin, flourishing his fist over a sea of cloth caps.

Mrs. Wahorska took Rose's arm and they slowly descended the grand staircase, which was still protected by sacking. At the bottom, in the places formerly occupied perhaps by flunkeys, five workmen were watching. One of them wore a paper hat like the Carpenter in 'Alice' and the others had embroidered skull caps. A sort of bloom of dust and whitewash lay over their hair and eyelashes and blond skin. They leaned back against the marble balustrade and watched step by step the descent of the girl in her smart foreign clothes and the bent shabby figure beside her. As they got nearer, Rose expected the workmen to smile or say good morning. They were as silent however as their prototypes in the photomural up above. It was certain they knew who the old lady was but it was of no importance to them, and the indifference, which had been handed out in this house through the generations, was being given back again with a long stare of their little pale eyes.

Twenty-three

'TODAY there is fish, that is because it is not Friday. No fish is allowed to be served in restaurants on Friday. You see, they are rather childish sometimes, the people who look after us.'

After this disquisition, the old lady went back to reading the menu, while Rose watched the surrounding tables. Next to them a delegation of Chinese, dressed like members of the Salvation Army, sat completely silent while a woman guide addressed them in squeaky English on the subject of industrial development. On the other side some shabby men in grey sweaters with zip-fasteners were talking German; beyond them was a group who looked like Arabs. There were little silk flags on the tables, unrecognizable, of recent countries. One table had no flag and there Adam Karpinski was sitting with two people. He gave no indication of having seen Rose.

Mrs. Wahorska began discussing the menu with Rose, who, agitated and hardly concentrating, found herself committed to herring in sour cream, beetroot soup, and chicken à la polonaise. After the fatigue of a morning of museums they came to an even quicker agreement that they should drink vodka.

Rose still wondered whether he had seen her or not. Among the confusion of languages in the restaurant, his

presence there tingled and throbbed like some sound just
above the range of the human ear.

Her back was turned to him, but he surely must have
noticed her when Mrs. Wahorska and she first arrived. If
he had, there might be some reason that had prevented
him from attracting her attention. The woman with him
was smart and not bad looking, the man squat and unattractive. Were they married? Intellectuals here got the
prettiest women, one had been told. Perhaps, however,
they were foreigners like herself, even though there was
no flag on their table.

The herring arrived, masked in its sauce of cream and
chopped onion, and with it the little carafe of vodka. They
drank to each other, and the old woman tasted the herring
appreciatively.

'That is good. You understand, we do not eat so well
on what we make by giving lessons and doing translations.
Also, every week I give something to the little nuns at
the convent.'

By the time cups of dark red soup were brought, the
old lady beamed and glistened: the luncheon was being
a success. As they drank another vodka, Rose heard Adam's
voice invade a moment of silence: he was speaking in
Polish, but for nearly a minute she could hear nothing
of what Mrs. Wahorska was saying.

'Afterwards my niece Halina will come here. She will
take you to see some more churches. The museums will
be closed, I think. Halina knows a great deal about our
churches, more than I. She is a nice girl but much too
serious, I am afraid. Not like my daughter, who is always
cheerful. But then, evidently I shall never see my daughter
again.' She blinked away a wave of unguarded emotion,
took up her glass again and fixed her gaze on Rose.

'And you, you are Catholic? That is strange for the English, I think.'

Rose was puzzled at this. This morning she had crossed herself going into the Cathedral by the Wawel palace; the sharp-eyed old woman had noticed it. Now Rose went rather pink, as she used to when explaining about this.

'My mother was a convert. When I was a child she sent me to a Convent school. It was during the war.'

'And you?' The improbable painted eyebrows were raised.

'My father wanted us to be free to choose.'

'And what have you chosen?'

'Nothing.'

Disapproval is middle class; the upper classes prefer to employ a sudden and complete loss of interest. Mrs. Wahorska began to attack the small chicken-half on her plate and the bowl of fresh cucumber beside it. Rose thought that she was about to speak again but when nothing came of these preparatory mumbles, which were due to nothing more than the violent tussle with fragile bones, she herself said: 'Of course, it is different here, I expect.'

'You are correct.' The old woman wiped her mouth and said fiercely: 'In Poland if we had lost our religion, we would have disappeared, we too. It defined us. Now they are taking it away from our children and they know what they are doing. We will disappear, we will become a part of Russia or perhaps a part of nowhere. Here we are not free to choose. We cannot choose a nothing.'

'I suppose not.' There were many objections to this totalitarian attitude but Rose was not in a position to make them. The lunch continued, with Rose no longer a person of much importance; she was rapidly demoralized by the sceptical smiles with which the old lady greeted her further attempts at conversation.

When Adam came out of the restaurant, Rose was sitting alone in the foyer of the hotel while Mrs. Wahorska telephoned her niece.

'You see, we must always meet. Krakow is like that.' He made a gesture of holding a clutch of eggs or a bird's nest. 'Are you having a nice time with that old thing?'

'No. Awful,' she said vehemently, and then felt guilty.

She hoped he would stay but already he was moving off.

'Don't let her bore you too much, will you?'

With this unhelpful remark, he left her; his two companions were already waiting in the car outside. Rose saw him go with a pang of loss. There was no prospect of escape from Mrs. Wahorska for another three days.

Rose was incredibly far from home, and now remorseful at leaving the Rudowskis and at launching out into an indefinite world of strangers. She should not have deserted them in the short time they would have of her in the whole of their lives, with so much that still needed straightening out. With all this in mind, she forced a bright smile at Mrs. Wahorska when she returned.

The other rejected this as the silliness of a person who lacked any interest to catch the attention. 'Halina will be here directly.'

They took up each other's company like a burden that had to be toted around for some reason forgotten to both of them.

Twenty-four

'*E* T *ce Monsieur Armstrong-Jones?*'

'Well, I don't—'

'Marysia Strelicka is now not minding so much her daughter marrying a man of no family. If the sister of the Queen of England may do it, you understand—'

Halina, the art-historian niece, had brought her guest to somebody's name-day party. It took place in a couple of tiny rooms, near some marshalling yards at the farthest edge of the city. The two rooms were crowded with elderly people, whose whiteish distinguished look, as though already partly of commemorative stone, made them seem remote from everything else. In fact, whether traditional academics or survivors of the pre-war aristocracy, they did their best to involve themselves at every opportunity with the arguments of the age: they wanted to feel that they were endangered and possibly dangerous. Because of this, though their lives were extremely hard, they were never bored.

Their hostess found no satisfaction in Rose's answers about the Royal Family and turned away. She was glad to have captured other visitors from outside the circle of a provincial town; the writer Bogdan Malczarek, recently returned from the West with his wife, who was rather less interesting; and Adam Karpinski from Warsaw, with flushed face and jabbing forefinger, holding forth to a group and expressing the exact mixture of knowledge and alarm, the painful bite down on to the rotten tooth of fact, which they all appreciated so much.

Though the writer's wife was not as pretty she had appeared to be at the hotel, her smart clothes and brightened skin and eyes distinguished her from the other guests. This glitter of distinction however was a surface result of Western productivity, for she turned out to be the saddest and least convinced of any of them. She had the cold whining voice sometimes found in conjunction with the East European intonation of English, and the moment she found herself with a foreigner she began to chant forth her litany of complaints. England came late on her list, when the little glasses had been refilled.

'You must forgive me but I did not like your country.'

'Oh, yes.'

'I was so unhappy there that I had to say to my husband, take me away or I shall probably be ill.' She had the exile's voice of talking endlessly about happiness, which she referred to as though it was her right, and everything had happened in conspiracy to keep her from it; they had not been received in English society, her husband had quarrelled with his fellow exiles over some political magazine or other. They had been obliged to work — she offered this bitterly to Rose, as something Rose herself would not dream of. But it had been impossible for her husband, who was a Doctor of Law, to find work and he disapproved of the job she was taking.

'In a bakery, imagine, with all sorts of low people. I had enough of England, I can tell you. I never see such ugly people, with such funny clothes like old peasant women. Whatever you can say, Krakow is better than Ealing.'

'Ealing?'

'We lived in Ealing, of course.' The woman stared out on to wild spaces of mania. They were left alone. Her troubles were too subjective to command any sympathy and the other guests avoided her. For many of them, she had been given the opportunity of freedom and failed and she was therefore uninteresting and even a little repulsive.

'Then we went to America. America is terrible. I was shocked, so shocked. We have lived there for twelve years but we do not like the people at all. And now my husband earns some money here with his books, so we are back here again.'

'And here?'

The woman lowered her voice. 'It is terrible, I cried my eyes out. But my husband wishes to stay.'

The long discussion on the other side of the room had been vehement but good natured. Everyone kept a respectful distance from the fierce conclusions such arguments seemed to hunt out: they were recognized and let go, and the participants returned to more tolerable themes. At length Adam was able to join Rose. He lowered himself heavily on to the divan beside her, a little glorified by drink and flushed with the excitement of the hunt.

'What was all that about?'

'You know what it was all about. Miss Rose — may I please call you Rose? You know now, don't you?' Tears came into his eyes. 'You can tell them about what has happened to us, the terrible things that have been done to us.'

She watched him as though about to pick lint off his coat, and was fascinated again at the curious combination of melancholy and extreme high spirits.

While they were walking home, Halina said: 'She is

exactly like the Ancient Mariner. She must tell her story
to everybody that she meets. It is the tragedy about our
people who are scattered. We feel that it is too late now,
and we can have no more contact with them, which is
very sad because they are our own people.'

'Perhaps those two will stay here. She told me her
husband wanted to.'

'They will go, I think. They both have American passports still, you see, and they can travel whenever they like.
That is the worst thing for us — we have to stay here. We
would like to travel but it is not possible. We may only
travel when the Government says so. If they would allow us
that, it would still be bad, but not so bad. How long are
you in Krakow?'

'Well, I —'

'My husband and I would like you to come to our flat —'

'They — the writer and his wife invited me to go to
the mountains, you see.'

The big iron gate of the Wahorska town house loomed
up in front of them. Rain had fallen and the trees in the
ruined garden were dripping heavily. Beyond, everything
was silent, the city plunged early into medieval sleep. The
old lady had lent Rose a key to the inner door, and now
they went up the back stairs, with the Museum of the
Workers' Party silent and shuttered below them.

The old lady had been working on a translation. Her
eyes were dark rimmed and her skin white, almost trans-
parent-looking.

'They are very small people, from near Lwow, I think,'
she said, when she was told about the Malczareks.

'They invited me to go with them in their car, to the
mountains.'

'My dear, you have escaped well. They probably wish

to make use of you in some way or other. She is a very tedious woman and I believe partly Jewish.'

Because the niece did not speak French, the conversation was triangular and awkward. Now Rose had to appeal to her for help.

'Of course you must go. You must see as much as you can of our country.'

A long interchange ensued between Mrs. Wahorska and Halina. The news that the English girl really wanted to go with the Malczareks, small people as they were, came as a personal affront; the old lady felt she was being abandoned, her hospitality rejected. This feeling she must have acquired and enjoyed for its own sake, since she showed no violent affection for her guest. Rose wondered whether Halina was embroidering the situation with any other reasons. She listened hard for Adam's name or some word that might mean he was being brought into the conversation. But her effort was unrewarded.

The women turned to her. Their faces were businesslike and unsmiling.

'It is settled then. When do they leave?'

'Tomorrow morning.'

At this the old lady appeared to be offended further.

Rose was sorry for her, not liking her much but as usual disarmed by the perpetual defeat. Perhaps that miasma hung thicker over Krakow than either Warsaw or Biala Gora. Escape in a fast car into the emptiness of woods and fields would be the only way to restore anyone's spirits.

Twenty-five

FLYING back to Biala Gora, Rose stopped for only two hours and spent them walking up and down in Warsaw Airport, happy with her thoughts and only mildly disconsolate at having finished her last detective story. Again the aeroplane wheeled up out of the drab city, the Palace of Culture spun round half-obscured by flocculent cloud, but now the feelings she had towards all of this were changed. Everything had meaning, each sight was a word in a great poetical tragedy and once you had learned this you could not cease from gazing with devouring eyes.

Tadeusz was waiting for her, in exactly the same place that he had waited on her first evening in Poland, which was now so long ago. The sight of him once more, all that youth and intensity, was almost insupportable, and her eyes filled with tears.

'You have a good trip?'

'I've had a wonderful time. Everybody has been wonderful.'

Of course there was nothing at all she could tell him and instead she turned on him a face of such radiance that he shivered, excited already. He wondered, too, why she was crying.

'I love your country, you know, Tadeusz. I really do.'

If Mark Tatham had told her that at that moment she was echoing the drunken Miss Handisyde, who had been at lunch on the first day, she would have denied it with violence. She was not drunk but in love. The world spun round, then settled.

'You saw Wawel? And Zakopane?'

'Everything.' Already Tadeusz had picked up her suitcases. 'No. This time we are taking a taxi. I simply insist.'

'All right. I catch one.'

He ran off. Rose was alone. It was growing dark and for a moment the meaning fled out of everything. The street and buildings assumed a matt, dead look, like an old photograph.

When he returned in the taxi, Rose at last remembered to ask: 'How are Mummy and Papa?'

'All right.' He frowned. 'I will tell you.'

As the taxi drove off, he said quickly. 'I think they are worried because two men were coming to our house asking about the Englishman.'

'What Englishman?'

'The one you know.'

'You mean Der—'

He clapped a hand on her mouth, nodding his head toward the taxi driver's shoulders.

'Who came?'

'You know who I mean.'

The walls and bare trees fled back. By now Rose and Tadeusz had become excited and conspiratorial, in an easy and unavoidable way. He smirked for a moment and then said in a high voice: 'I think taxi drivers are very nice people.'

No tremor to indicate understanding came from the shoulders in front.

'They sometimes do understand, you know. It is because they were in England in the war.'

Silence, while they thought about that distant, empty time, and what it had done to their lives.

'Go on about these men.'

'It was the Police. At least not the Police — you know who.' He made two letters with his fingers.

'But why?' She was startled and drawn-looking.

'Papa thinks he was selling things on the Black Market. Do you think so?'

'Perhaps. He isn't very intelligent.'

'Mummy said he was an oik.'

Rose turned away. 'Oh God. Really!'

A little later the taxi driver suddenly spoke. She jumped with fright and Tadeusz grinned; they had already voted the driver incapable of speech and this was as miraculous as if part of the engine had given tongue. But when it turned out to be Polish, her excitement dwindled down to mere apprehension. Tadeusz however carried on an intent conversation which lasted until they had drawn up outside the block of flats.

'I told him you were English. He thought you might be German. He has an uncle in Chicago. So now I knew he did not understand anything we were talking about.'

'Just what were we talking about? Who was it who came?'

'The U.B. The Secret Police.'

'About Derek Loasby?'

'Yes.'

Overhead a flock of pigeons was wheeling round in the last sunlight that could seep through the industrial haze. In Krakow the past continued into the present, but living here in Biala Gora was like recolonizing a dead planet, fearfully camping out in an unfinished world. She followed Tadeusz up the cinderpath.

It was all very like her first evening in Poland except that Janet and Witek both greeted her. They trusted her now.

Rose, although now quite untrustworthy, was no longer a wincing stranger. She found them happier than she had feared. Of course it is when you concentrate on people that their difficulties appear insoluble. Now she could only give them a part of her attention. Work-worn, small, greyish and smiling, the Rudowskis appeared to belong together.

They were disunited, however, over the problem of Derek Loasby.

'Elzbieta Barcik gives him Polish lessons, and he told her they wanted to see him. She thought it was because of Black Marketing. He goes round with all sorts of students and perhaps they've got him into trouble.'

'But they like him. He's lots of friends.'

'The students get all sorts of pressures on them. Ask Witek.'

Witek listened in silence, to indicate that the problem was purely an English one. 'They are young and some of them have not good backgrounds. I am surprised that the Englishman should do this. We are told always that they have high social morality.'

'They do,' Janet said. 'In England.'

Rose was more doubtful. 'He's very unsure of himself and he might easily do something silly, if the others asked him to.'

'Please, silly?'

'Something about money.'

'Speculation is a grave social problem.'

The sisters tried to ignore him.

'What did They come here for?'

'Who told you?' Janet asked.

'Tadeusz, of course.'

Witek shifted about and then said: 'I am sorry that Tadeusz has told you of this. There are still some aspects which a foreigner may find that it is difficult —'

'Oh, Witek. Please! I *am* grown up.'

This was the first time she had lost patience with him and her voice sounded exactly like Janet's. The small movements of his body checked and became total stillness. The hurt sliced through his eyes, leaving them wounded and terrible, and then he got up very slowly and walked out of the room.

'I — I'm sorry about that.'

'It doesn't matter,' Janet said fumbling for a cigarette.

'How are things?'

'We have our ups and downs, but things are going better on the whole. Luckily he wasn't here when they came round. They wanted to know how we met Loasby. I said he had only been here twice. Hala brought him when he first arrived. Then you. You know I didn't like him.'

'Yes. You told me.'

'It was a shock when they came. Like going back to Stalin's time. You see, nowadays we can live from day to day without knowing about all this.' The match flame quivered in Janet's hand. She shook it out. 'I was terribly worried about the passport.'

'Janet, what do you really want to do?'

'I want to get Tadeusz away from all this. For ever.'

'But you?'

'I don't matter, my life's finished.' She blew out smoke and watched Rose. 'Tadeusz must go.'

Rose's face was screwed up with anxiety. 'I'm sure you're wrong. I've travelled about now and I've come to my own conclusions. However bad it may seem, and is, there are so many things to be done here and people to fight for them. A man has to decide this.'

'You can't ask Witek to decide —'

'I meant Tadeusz —' Before she could continue, the telephone started ringing.

'He wants to speak to you. Be careful what you say.'

'Who?' Rose rushed and grabbed the receiver. But it was only Derek Loasby.

Twenty-six

BECAUSE of the rain, every table in the café was filled. Derek stood outside and was dripped on, and had the usual feeling that rain fell, not alike on the just and unjust, but only on the incompetent. After five minutes the rain was just another aspect of his preoccupation, his sense of the extremeness of life, which kept him bouncing from foot to foot and whistling between his teeth. He was doing exactly this when Rose found him.

'Derek. Hullo.'

He rushed at her as though he had loved her for years, brought himself up short, slipped and almost fell on his thick rubber soles, still holding her hand. She smiled, blinking the rain away.

'Let's find somewhere to sit,' Rose said, 'And then you can tell me all about it.'

'Then you know?'

She looked past him into the crowded café. 'There doesn't seem to be any room.'

He muttered something and steered her out through the rain and into another doorway.

'What did you say?'

'Any port in a storm.' He sounded desperate.

'Yes. I suppose so.'

The place they had now entered had the willed squalor of Slav drink shops. They stopped, feeling already half smothered by the odours of sour beer and rank bodies. The rain, however, still fell in a solid cascade behind them. Everyone was staring at them and so they sat down, both nervous, at a small table in the middle of the room. At first they did not look at each other; their eyes wandered but soon returned. This squalor seemed exhibitionistic, a denial of anything but the bed-rock upon which life scrabbled to survive.

Even before a youth had put two glass-stoppered bottles and two smeared tumblers before them the effect of all this went a little to their heads; they were young and it gave them so strong a feeling of pioneering, of being where nobody had been before. She smiled at him quite gaily and he was ready to forget everything they were here for.

'Well?'

After this bleak word, he was careful. 'What have they been saying about me?'

'It's that Miss Thing—the one who blinks and teaches you Polish—she said something to Janet. And Janet—'

He gave a patient sigh which suggested that he was more important than all this. 'I haven't told *her* anything.'

Rose was beginning again, when he drank some beer and spluttered. He really was in a violently nervous state, like somebody who has taken Benzedrine.

'I'm sorry about dragging you into this. But there wasn't anybody else to tell. I heard you were away so I waited till you came back.'

Rose realized from this that, rather humbly, he respected her judgment. 'Don't worry about me. Anyway, I—'

'I don't feel I can trust anybody.'

'Derek, what is this all about?'

'They've asked me to stay on, you see.' His fingers

F

drummed up and down on the table. His smile was triumphant, and crafty.

'Is it something about your scholarship?'

'No, no.' He shook his head until his cheeks clicked. 'To come over, to work here — like those Missing Diplomats and people. They offered me a job. Not much money, but their standards are different. Girls, too.'

'What girls?'

'They said there were a lot of nice girls here. I said I knew.'

They were off on the wrong subject again. They guessed that both had felt the sexual touch of the place but the evidence was inadmissible to this conversation.

She tapped at her cigarette thoughtfully. 'Janet and Witek thought the trouble was that you were selling things.'

'That's what I thought.'

'You mean you were?'

'Of course. I told you, you remember. Everyone does here, they keep asking you. Then I found I was being watched.' His face warmed through like an electric fire. 'This bit makes me look rather foolish. You remember that girl Wanda, I think you met her? Well, I left her in my room while I went to get cigarettes and half-way down the stairs I found I'd forgotten my money so I went back and when I opened the door I saw she was going through my letters.'

'But Derek, people often do that.'

'Jotting things down. On a little pad.'

Rose half-closed her eyes and giggled. 'Just trying to improve her English.'

'Wanda doesn't know any English,' he wailed. 'She's always said so.'

'What did you do?' Rose was still laughing.

'Nothing.'

That this was untrue was obvious to both of them. He would have had to do something. But he disliked being teased and at present it muddled him. He stared down at the dirt-engrained table between the beer glasses and his mind flicked over a succession of sore but not entirely disagreeable points, which were the recollection of what in fact had taken place, and he felt again the shock of Wanda standing there by the desk, reading a letter from his mother.

He had retreated quickly, slammed the front door so that the chain rattled, and returned to the room to find her lying, unsmiling but self-consciously posed across the folk-weave cover of his bed. Syntax deserted him, and he could only remember the single word 'money'. '*Pieniądze,*' he blurted out, rummaged for his wallet and fled. In the race to the kiosk and back up the dingy staircase he had thought of nothing at all. But when he saw her again Wanda had become a thing. He could not bring himself to speak to her. She did not drink in the daytime, she had already heard all his gramophone records, and soon she finished her cigarette and still lay there. . . . This memory he carried around with him like a somewhat grubby handkerchief. Her treachery might have made him incapable but at that point it had excited him extremely.

'I didn't do anything,' he lied. 'I want them to learn to trust me.'

'But you don't trust them.'

'I suppose I don't.' His attention wandered. It was impossible to tell what he was after, beyond convincing himself of his own importance.

'Does Mirek know about this?'

'Who?'

'Mirek Sypniewski. Your friend. Haven't I got his name right?'

'Oh, yes, Mirek.' Loasby fiddled with the ash tray and said: 'No. I don't trust Mirek at all.'

'Really, I think you must have persecution mania or something. He was frightfully outspoken against anything like that. And, after his experience, he must know all about it.'

'That's the trouble, isn't it? They've got something on him. In any case he is always coming into contact with foreigners. No, I don't trust old Mirek any further than I can throw him.'

She felt obscurely wounded by this. Mirek Sypniewski had been the first person here really to catch her sympathy. She remembered him standing in the dark, heavy with sadness. To distrust him would be cruel, and yet it might be more cruel to expect too much. He was not after all a noble survivor from the past, like Adam Karpinski, but a product of this generation.

Rose stood up.

'Let's go. This beer's horrid and I think it's stopped raining.'

A few slow sun-refracting drops were falling but there was a lifted clearness in the air. At four o'clock the streets were crowded with workers going home to dinner. The shop windows were filled with the usual unrealities, plaster models of legs of pork and salami and photographs of Gomulka for May Day, surrounded with whirls of scarlet and crêpe paper, and in reaction to this, though most people were wrapped up in sick-smelling plastic against the weather, they had armed themselves with something real to carry home: a loaf of bread, shiny with freshness, or a spray of pussy-willow or apple blossom or a bunch of marsh marigolds.

In this crowd Derek and Rose were soon embarrassed by each other. Each of them wanting to get back to their own Poles and if they spent too much time together they felt diminished and anxious.

Because of this they walked in silence, both listening to the relentless squeals of Derek's new Polish shoes, until Rose said:

'What I was trying to tell you was, that two men came to the flat and asked about you.'

'What did they look like?'

'It was while I was away. The Rudowskis were worried because Tadeusz is trying to get a passport.'

Her Poles, however, did not bother him. 'What did the men say?'

'They asked about you. Janet didn't know too much.'

'Probably they were the same ones. They really are interested in me. They know there are certain things I approve of a lot.'

'Like being spied on.'

'No. Not that.'

Yet he went around administering approval, and was snubbed for it, though less often than he should have been. Only yesterday he had complimented somebody on the cleanness of the streets; 'Yes, we Poles have so little we can afford to throw away.' Today he noticed for the first time the new municipal wastepaper baskets, which took the impractical form of penguins with gaping beaks. 'Just look at those.'

'They're hideous, aren't they?'

He was hurt: if an effort was being made, Rose ought not to be beastly about it.

'At least they're *doing* something,' he said.

At the tram stop, he told her that his new friends had asked to see him again.

'Will you go?'

'What do you think?'

'I think it would be rather stupid. What good can it do you? Or them, for that matter. Besides, I think you ought to tell somebody. Other English students'll be coming here, won't they?'

He shrugged his shoulders. 'Who'll I tell?'

'Our Embassy.'

He sniffed. 'A lot of snobs. What do they know about real conditions here? They live apart, cut off.'

'You could tell them, then.'

'I could write a report, I suppose. For the Ambassador.'

'You don't need to do that,' Rose said, feeling tired by now. 'One of them is coming down next week. I'll put him on to you.'

'Oh, all right.' Derek looked gloomy. His glory was being dissipated all too rapidly.

Rose was sorry for him: 'Look, why don't you come out to supper tonight?'

After listening to him for over an hour, it was really almost too much for her patience to watch him weigh up this invitation against his other opportunities for this evening.

'All right,' he said. Then the tram she was waiting for came swinging round the loop in front of them.

Rather later Derek turned up at the Rudowskis' flat, where he drank too much of Witold's *jarzembiak* and gave a curiously confused account of the possibilities of English life.

'Unless you're in with the Establishment,' he kept repeating, 'You haven't really got a chance.'

After he had gone, Tadeusz asked Rose: 'Is it true what he said?'

'Of course it's not true,' Janet told him. 'He's one of those people who like to blame others for their own failure.'

'I found his point of view most interesting,' Witold said.

Twenty-seven

THE following day Rose received the telephone call she was expecting.

'My darling Miss Rose, may we meet very soon?'

'All right.'

'Now?'

A pause. Adam sensed people standing round her and even pictured the stupid Rudowski breathing on her neck.

'All right, yes.'

Adam replaced the telephone and went back to his table.

He had spent the morning at the University, in conversation with a few of the old professors who still retained the glamour which attached to learning in this country. Most of these were survivors from Lwow and Wilno, the lost universities in the East. A good deal of their glory had departed, nowadays they were bald, their features were adorned with every type of wrinkle and protuberance, they were dressed often in garments of what looked like old furnishing material; they remained however both happy and civil. They still had the relish of their obscure knowledge (one of them, Professor Doctor Boczok, spoke all the Melanesian languages but had never left Europe). Regularly they published the results of their research. They had discovered that even in the worst times only one paragraph of a learned article need to be devoted to the ritual *Ave Caesar*; if the article were to be published in the United States, this paragraph could be excised.

But these graceful and antiquated professors could seldom be got at by themselves. A henchman was always present, an assistant of either sex, bloodless and bespectacled, whose sense of reality was so feeble that it could be satisfied by the latest efforts to make Marxism fit the facts. These poor specimens considered themselves Adam Karpinski's enemies: they were supporters of Witold Rudowski.

Adam did not let them worry him. It was pleasanter to think about Rose, who now came into the café. She was wearing a simple charcoal-coloured dress and had her hair done up in a sort of bun. He kissed her hand, then her face.

She settled beside him. In both of them the insistent machinery of strain was suddenly switched off; everything was calm now and there was nothing to worry about any more. While Adam ordered coffee, her eyes began to absorb him again. Dirt ringed his shirt collar. He smelt quite different from in the mountains. He looked so smashed, she ached with love for him.

From the five days they had already spent together, she had learned the course of the syndrome. First there had been the wild elation, the race in the growling Mercedes towards the snowfields. Adam sat half-turned in the seat beside Bogdan Malczarek, who was driving, and talked continuously. At such times Adam dominated everything; merely by being there he ridiculed the querulous plain-song of Mrs. Malczarek, who once they were out of Krakow became calm and cheerful. Beyond the car windows the sloping landscapes were an unending celebration. The river glittered between new-budded trees, wooden houses were

F*

being built, fields were being ploughed. Then the mountains closed in, and in the villages the foreign car was stared at by strange men who wore white felt trousers, elaborately embroidered, and girl-guide hats ringed with cowrie shells.

At Adam's instigation, the writer threw the long black car like a racing toboggan down the thawed roads. Towards evening they came to the rest house where they were to stay. It was sparsely furnished and decorated only with such battered hunting trophies from the past as a stuffed lynx and a frieze of roebuck antlers, or perhaps chamois horns, like little coat-hooks all the way up the stairs. '*Vous voyez,*' Adam said at the sight of these, '*On a été diablement cocu ici.* What's that in English?'

'Cuckolded, I suppose. . . .'

And now, back in Biala Gora, Rose laughed.

'Why are you laughing?'

'I was remembering the little horns.'

He sighed, swinging her hand in his. 'If one could always live in the mountains, one's life might be bearable.'

'Please don't.'

He shook his head. 'You will go away and why should I wish to survive? I don't really want to survive as far as tomorrow, when Mr. Mark and Mrs. Alexandra will arrive. She is a bitch and a cow, Alexandra, and a terrible liar. I adore her. Tell me what on earth can the Tathams think about us?'

'Us?'

'Poles.'

'Oh.'

From the depressive phase of the syndrome, women and outsiders were excluded.

In the mountains, this phase had followed on the third

or fourth day. Rose had sat with him all one afternoon by a stream burning-cold from the glaciers, while he talked about the trains beyond the Urals, the camp and the Kolkhoz, and his wanderings after the amnesty. Tears scorched her eyes, though it was all long ago and those never released must be dead by now. Bones in the permafrost.

The phase returned now. 'We are infected with unhappiness. Our position is an impossible one. It would be much better if we had been all exterminated. It was a good idea last time but it did not quite succeed. The next time, which will be quite soon now, they will be successful and we Poles will not trouble the rest of the world any more.'

She tried to ride this one out but could not. 'Oh, please. Stop. Stop.'

'What difference does it make to you, Rose? Already you say to me you are leaving—'

'Stop, please,' she sobbed.

He stopped, but only to plunge into a malodorous silence like a sick animal.

After about five minutes of this, she asked plaintively: 'Can't we go and have lunch somewhere? I'm so hungry.'

They went to the restaurant of the Hotel Hoffman, a huge room with galleries and a round glass roof, built in a kind of Baltic baroque style which was now coated all over with sour-cream paint. 'There is nowhere else to eat in this dreadful town,' Adam said. They sat at a square table with a dirty white cloth and two bottles of mineral water.

On reading the menu, however, he became livelier.

'Wonderful! They have *pstrag*.'

'What on earth's that?'

'In English, I forget. A fish.'

'It's usually carp.'

'No, no. *Forelle.*'

He began to sing in a cheerful baritone and when he
had stopped they ordered the cold trout and some fillet
of beef *en croûte*. This last too was only to be found by
occasional good fortune, since in a people's democracy
all parts of the animal appear to carry much the same
value. Their order was discussed at some length with the
waiter and when he had gone Rose asked: 'Do you always
call waiters "darling"?'

'Warsaw people do.' He looked around him appraisingly.
'Perhaps it is not so bad here. I am glad because I shall
be coming here quite often.'

It was bleakly tactless of him to speak of a time when
she would have gone. 'Why?'

'When I have my job at the University.'

'But I thought Witek —'

Adam hunched forward. He was intent, not with personal affection, but with the effort of proving his arguments. His grey eyes looked deep into her eyes and walked
about on the bottom of her soul.

'Now, darling,' he said, 'he is quite impossible, isn't he?'

'No! No! Please don't say that. I *have* to believe in
my own people.'

'Poor Rose.' He curled his hands with pity.

'What has happened? He seemed to think it was so
certain.'

Adam's breath brushed over her face. 'You know that
I have had some political difficulties in the past. But this
morning I learn that our Party is in a liberal mood just
now. So I think I shall be accepted after all.'

'You don't even live here!'

'I shall come down once a fortnight to give my lectures.'

'You couldn't do that in England.'

'No, you couldn't do that in England. Tell me, does your dear brother-in-law actually know anything? I have never been able to find out.'

'Poor Witek. He'll lose everything.'

'Everything?'

'Yes.' She stared away in whirling misery for some minutes. Then she swallowed some vodka. 'Well, let's try and be happy and not worry about my family.'

'Darling, you should be like me and have no family. It is very fashionable here since the war. Even my wife has stopped writing to me.'

The waiter served them with trout in aspic from a long metal dish. Adam picked up two forks and stared at his plate for a few minutes. Then he looked up, as though he had just thought of something.

'Rose, why do you stay here? Why don't you come to Warsaw? You have three weeks left.'

'Have I?' she asked with surprise.

'Yes.' He removed a bone from his mouth and put it on the side of his plate. 'I saw your weezer.'

'My *what*?'

'Your weezer. On your passport.'

'My visa!'

It was the first proper mistake in English she had heard him make, and she giggled a touch hysterically, even though she saw it annoyed him. 'When?'

'What do you mean when?'

'When did you look at my visa?'

'When you gave them your passport at the rest house, of course.' He tapped the table impatiently. 'Will you come to Warsaw?'

'It's all so difficult.'

'What do you mean, it's so difficult? You can do what you want.'

'Darling, how can I possibly know what I want? I simply can't let them down.'

'Of course you can, you simply do not care. You are cold and trivial like all the English.'

'You know that is not true.'

'Then after this I shall never see you again?'

She looked away. Perhaps she could not imagine this yet and thus could stand it.

'You'll come to luncheon tomorrow with Alexandra and Mark? Please. It will be insupportable without you.'

'It's getting difficult to explain at home.'

'Stop talking about those ridiculous people!' he shouted at her.

They finished their trout in a reverberating silence. While the plates were being changed, she picked up her vodka glass and said nervously: *'Na zdrowie!'*

'And, darling, do stop trying to cheer me up! Polish women let their men be gloomy.'

'Sorry.'

'Never mind.'

He smiled wanly. At that moment he looked so smashed that it was difficult to believe that, in Warsaw, he was a successful man who held down three jobs.

When they left the restaurant he said: 'Now we take a tram.'

The tram wound through the grey streets and went clear of the town. It was the same one that Rose had taken with Tadeusz but today she had forgotten this, being involved in a haze of sunlight and vodka and unhappy love.

'This,' Adam said, 'is the true contemporary problem. Nowhere to make love, except the middle of the forest.'

Twenty-eight

'I'M going to be out again, tonight.'
Janet was correcting a translation. She looked much older when she wore her spectacles. 'I thought you would be.'

'What do you mean?'

'Rose, it's difficult to keep secrets here. Mrs. Wahorska wrote from Krakow at once to Krystyna Kazimierska.'

'Those old bitches. They've always got their knife into somebody.'

'You're quite wrong, darling. In fact, entirely the opposite. They derive a tremendous kick out of the whole thing. Besides, Krystyna adores him, she can never stop talking about him and old "Sir Gawain and the Green Knight".'

Janet crossed out a word, consulted a technical dictionary on the table beside her, and wrote in another word. 'I'm getting to be such an expert on steel-processing, you can't imagine.' She chewed her pencil a moment. 'The only mistake you can make is to marry them. Then you lose caste absolutely.'

'He's married already.'

'Separated.'

'Catholic,' Rose said.

'I suppose so. You've got something stuck in your hair.'

Rose put up her hand. 'A pine-needle.' She giggled. 'He might have told me. Oh dear, it's all so wonderful.'

'Are you going to tell that to the lawyers?'

'No. I suppose not.'

'What are you going to tell them? You haven't got so long, you know.'

'I know. But I can't think now. I must change. He's waiting for me outside. I couldn't bring him in in case Witek was here. By the way, does Witek know about this?'

'I shouldn't think so. He has no one to tell him. You would be in hot water, then.'

'All these lies. But we've always told lies in our family, haven't we?'

Janet flinched: truth such as this one, certainly, had been avoided at Barnham.

Adam was standing at the nearest tram stop. He still wore his raincoat, although the evening was fine and the wide sky over the plain was pale and translucent, with two storks flying across it.

The rain had held off during the past week now, horses and carts came in from the country covered with dust, and the ground underfoot was beginning to turn into dust. But near the beer kiosk, all the beer that had tilted out of glasses held by contented peasants and soldiers formed into a fine sour mud, which squelched gently under their unsteady feet.

'At last! What a horrible place to live!'

'It isn't so bad.'

By now her eye had grown selective and, from the dull background of apartment buildings and *terrains vagues*, picked out the lame soldier summoning his tumbler pigeons out of the walnut-tree, the young couples in bright cotton sitting among the clumps of weeds. This evening the three boys who shared a motor-bicycle had taken it completely to pieces, and stood round marvelling at the pleasure of something entirely their own.

'For me, it is terrible! Such people! ' Adam said.

'They're perfectly ordinary people.'

'Perfectly ordinary! Warsaw people don't have such faces! '

She looked to see the joke and saw he was entirely serious.

That evening, they wandered round the town. They had an unsuccessful meal at the railway station. After sunset, rather late, they ended up at the Students' Cellar.

At first there was nobody Rose recognized: of the feral young men with bad teeth and dirty sweaters, any one might have been Mirek Sypniewski but none was. Among the girls, though, she noticed Loasby's friend Wanda, standing alone. The girl was wearing a pink sack dress, fierce against her raw complexion. The misfortune in her appearance somehow made it certain that Derek was not far away.

And indeed, while Adam was fetching glasses of wine, he came sidling up.

'I haven't seen Them again,' he said. 'But I've learned a lot since I saw you.'

'Ought you to talk about it here? '

He darkened — the spectral light in the cellar made his blushes grey — and lowered his voice. 'That girl — you remember I told you? '

'She's just over there, Derek.'

'I know.'

While Derek continued talking, Rose watched the girl who leaned against the opposite wall of the cellar. Quite evidently she was in a depressed state: whenever anybody spoke to her, she did not answer but jerked away as if she had physically been bumped into.

'I chucked her, you won't be surprised to hear. I mean,

it was impossible after that business of reading my letters. Funnily enough as soon as I did, people started telling me all sorts of things about her. Apparently two years ago she was trying to get to England, we wouldn't give her a visa because she was an orphan and since then she's been trying to get off with any foreigner who comes around. That was why she took up with me in the first place —'

'This is Derek Loasby, Adam Karpinski.'

Derek's eyes reached conclusions, his face candidly summed it all up, he even half-nodded. He offered cigarettes, and lolled back in his chair, and ten minutes later he was still with them. Rose simmered with irritation. The thought of the English was slightly repulsive to her now, half-raw and embryonic as they were; this particular specimen, roaming at large with his self-complacency in the area of pain, gave special reason for feeling ashamed. If there was such a thing as commonness of soul, it was his.

Derek looked from Adam back to Rose. To him she wore a completely English look, with her clear skin and petulant mouth. He believed you could not interest her except by shock.

Abruptly he said: 'I'm leaving.'

'Goodnight, Derek.'

'No, no.' His hands tortured a cigarette pack. 'Really leaving. I could stay on but somehow I've lost interest here. Everything's got so messy, I can't concentrate any longer. You know how there's a time in a foreign country when you simply can't stand anything, any aspect of the place any more?'

Adam asked him a few civil questions about the work he was doing and the people he knew, but it was no use. Derek twisted about, exaggerated and lied. His sensibilities were scorched by the blaze of too much experience; not the experience of action, but of intention, the heavy pressure of future and past in this marginal place.

Finally he stood up and shook hands with Adam and then Rose. Rose said: 'I understand what you were talking about. But shouldn't you learn to forgive people and trust them?'

'How can I trust them?' the young man asked plaintively. He disappeared into the crowd of dancers.

Twenty-nine

'So there we are,' said Rose.

Mark Tatham, who was walking beside her in the public garden, paced more slowly.

'What do you think?' she asked.

'Since you've got the father's permission to take the boy to England, isn't it all right?'

'I hope so.'

By now they were at the statue of the poet Kochanowski, in front of the University. They could have been seen by Witek from his office window, but at this moment his head was bowed into the intracicies of his broken tape-recorder: when he looked up it was only to worry out the technical terms from the German brochure. He loved machinery and would have spent his life with it, had it not been for the greater prestige involved in academic life.

Alexandra was visiting an aged princess, an aunt of Krysia Kazimierska, who was holed up in a tiny room somewhere on the outskirts of the city.

The sun shone on the budding trees, on the sellers of strings of pretzels, sprinkled with rock-salt, which people munched to stave off hunger. Old men basked in rows on the park benches. The inhabitants of Biala Gora looked especially unprosperous in their weekday clothes. The English people seemed extraordinarily out of place, and every now and then an incredulous stare came towards them from one of the bleak old faces on the benches. A bunch of workmen gave Rose surprised smiles, not just of sexual appreciation but of pleasure at whatever had happened to bring so exotic a figure to this town.

'There won't be any difficulty about the visa?'

'I don't see why there should be. As long as you send him back.'

'Of course.' Now her footsteps went a little faster, pecking the asphalt among the courting pigeons; she saw, in spite of everything, some happiness ahead. 'Thank you, Mark.'

'Nothing to do with me at all. But you must be sensible, you know, Rose.'

Rose was being belittled by this. 'Why?'

'He is certain to find out about the money quite soon.'

'Oh no. We've told nobody. I don't see how he could find out. No, what we must do is wait.'

He smiled. 'What for, Rose?'

'For — for Tadeusz to grow up. For the Cold War to — well, you know.' Her voice trailed off, because he was still smiling and such hopes always appeared feeble, even on the sunniest mornings here.

A cluster of students went by them on their way to lectures in the main building of the University. The pony-tailed girls, the awkward and intense young men were all talking at once; caught up in the swirling air of ideas and feelings, they sounded like a rookery in full cry. The smile faded from Mark's face and he looked appalled. He really is pompous, Rose thought.

'And this student?' he asked.

'Which student?'

'Loasby. He came to see me this morning. The whole business seems rather a muddle. Does he really want to marry this girl?'

Rose squeaked. 'No. Of course not.'

'That's what he said.'

'He must be stark staring. Only last night he was saying the most frightful things about her.'

'Evidently there was a grand reconciliation.' The distaste stiffened his face. 'Have you seen her?'

'Yes. I don't know what she's like though. She doesn't speak English. A bit cross-looking I thought, but that may indicate banked-down fires.'

Evidently Mark did not need this information. He did not ask for opinions or give them.

She wondered how much Derek had told him. Derek might be involved in promises and complications which he was ashamed of and which, for various social reasons, he could never confess to anybody like Mark. He was desperate to interest people, had probably only come to Biala Gora in the first place to make himself more interesting, but it would be no use with Mark. Derek was a raw clumsy person but one did not like to think of him as irretrievably in a jam.

Mark looked at his watch. 'Let's go in and have a drink. We've brought down some whisky.'

'All right.'

'Only be careful what you say at the hotel. Our room's probably wired up like a telephone exchange.'

'All right.'

A warning like this brought a mixture of feelings now, no longer just the discomfort of living in a world of suspicion. It was like a comment on the physical deformity of someone dearly loved. Those she did love, Adam, Tadeusz and even Witek, could have made this comment as easily as Mark did. But then they were sufferers; since Mark was immune, he ought not to blame.

Thirty

THE hotel was not far away. Just as they reached it a taxi drew up, and Alexandra was in it, with Adam seated beside her. It was a slight surprise to Rose because he had not mentioned he would be with Alexandra.

In Alexandra's presence, though, any such speculations were quickly forgotten. Her bell-voice rang out to greet Rose, whom she kissed. Adam hustled them briskly into the hotel and informed them that, since the restaurant service was so slow, there would be no time for a drink upstairs. Adam was quite altered when Alexandra was there and so was Mark. It was like having a wireless turned up: everyone had to talk a little louder, push a little harder. Or else, as Rose did now, keep silence.

Adam proved correct, and in spite of his efforts, and perhaps because of the Western air of assurance the four of them exuded among all those drab trade delegates, their lunch was interminably delayed. For long periods their tablecloth was adorned only with clogged ash-trays, and vodka and mineral-water glasses; the carafe of crystalline spirit waited in a frost-bloomed bucket beside it. The tables were small, though so widely separated in the huge room that you were out of earshot of your neighbours. They had to sit very close together; feet and knees, not immediately recognizable, bumped under the table; above it, Alexandra was the brightest and biggest. The vodka made her eyes sparkle but in any case her tongue was already loosened. She was in fine fig and blossoming with her pregnancy. Perhaps it was the complete lack of compassion in her voice which gave what she said the feeling of wit; her sense of timing was superb and the indiscretions she let out were fairly venial ones: the boring behaviour of United States Embassy wives, the antics of a South American minister in pursuit of the younger members of the League of Socialist Youth. Mark managed to sit through this with only a slight expression of constraint and the occasional interpolation of a mild 'darling!' Meanwhile Adam was echo and chorus and stimulus to everything she said. Like Krysia Kazimierska and her friends, he found any proof that people continued with their ludicrous behaviour was an assertion of life.

Not, however, if they were Poles. When Alexandra turned on any of his compatriots, she always was wrong. 'He may seem like that to you,' he would tell her, 'but he's a brilliant fellow,' and Alexandra always replied: 'Of course, Adam, I'm sure he's marvellous.' For himself Adam permitted quite different judgments: the political set-up was composed of conspirators and swine. But even then his attack never coincided with Alexandra's. He was out to dispraise when she praised, to commend where she chose to denigrate. It was like a game of catch in which they turned and twisted in pursuit of each other and neither managed to hold the other. Even on this minor occasion, the tension and the impassable barrier had to be there.

Mark drank more than the rest of them, nourishing his boredom. It tugged at his sleepy eyelids and bleared his long face like the onset of a sneeze. He shifted in his chair, long-legged and uncomfortable, clutching his knees. He watched the others as though they were part of something he had been staring at for a long time, part of the *longueurs* of his ambition. Across him, Adam's gaze held Alexandra's, while she talked on and on. Alexandra dominated. She had not had much education and all the confidence of the upper class was needed for such set-to's with men on their own level. Of course, Adam said he adored her. Rose disliked her, felt herself diminished by her.

Mark murmured 'Darling!' once again at something of Alexandra's. His gaze flickered away to Rose. Their eyes met.

Rose was scared, and blushed. The boredom had gone from Mark's face and instead there was a glitter of malice there. He was beckoning to her to enter a conspiracy against the other two. Because of Adam she did not want any part of it, but suddenly she began to feel a good deal more cheerful about Alexandra.

They had finished the cups of beetroot soup. Adam grew serious. He had embarked on his usual discourse, his effort to draw his country's boundaries in the empyrean above the shifting lines history had always provided. Even Alexandra could not pursue him as far as this region. Later, when he was portentously comparing the nation to his favourite, Sir Gawain, summoned to a mysterious destiny by a headless figure out of myth, she only muttered: 'Bully for Sir Gawain!' Adam smiled awkwardly and Rose was anguished because he might not know what Alexandra meant. He might be made fun of and she could not help him, though she ached to touch him and touch him again.

She shot her hand over her glass as the waiter tried to refill it. Adam's glass was refilled: he upended it and went on talking. Ah, couldn't he see how boring he had become? 'People will not want to listen when Gomulka is saying that the blanket is not big enough to cover us all. They want to see the blanket flying up there, like the flag.'

Mark emitted a sort of plopping sound. A single word, unvoiced: 'Balls.'

Rose, the only one of them to hear it, felt his knee press against hers.

His eye followed a line down Rose's cheek and neck until he could spy out the warm corner above the collar bone, the little pit that fell between the breasts. Everything else retreated into a dim and echoing haze of alcohol, the clang of metal trays in the kitchen, the waiters' feet padding on the red drugget, the squeal of a door opening on to sunlight brilliant enough to make you sneeze.

When Mark emerged from this contemplation, Alexandra was watching him, fierce and nasty.

'Our car will be waiting for us,' Adam said at last.

And Mark: 'Rose, what a pity you can't come along with us.'

And Alexandra: 'Let's go upstairs and pee, shall we, Rose?'

Released at last from the necessary constraints of the hotel dining-room, Rose began to chatter unwisely.

She walked round the Tathams' suite, examining, with more attention than they deserved, the prints of old Biala Gora on the walls, fingering the ungainly pottery statuettes and squares of folk-weave which are the official decoration of such places. 'It's not too bad, really, is it?' She peered through the net curtains at the cobbled street below, then turned back and began to wander round the room again. 'I must admit I'm fascinated by the micr — you know. Where do you think they hide them?'

Alexandra did not answer.

Rose was crushed: she had made a tactless remark, perhaps one which would be recorded, if They were listening. Less assured, she crossed over to the brass bedstead. 'These mattresses are pretty hard, aren't they? Why do they always make them in three bits, so you always get the gap just underneath you? And this sort of eiderdown thing, either too hot or too cold.'

These remarks, too, were left to die out.

Alexandra, who was seated in front of a mirror, knew how to treat another person's effort at conversation as though it were an inevitable mechanical noise. She bent down and straightened a stocking.

Awkward and unwelcome, Rose hung on. It had been ridiculous to expect good will of any sort from Alexandra, and rather careless to have let herself into this position at all. But somehow a worse thing was that Adam and the Tathams were now going away and leaving her forsaken and stranded in Biala Gora. It was not flattering to the Rudowskis to think this, but it seemed to be true.

Alexandra stood up and looked out of the window.

'Adam is waiting for Mark and me,' she said. It was the only thing she said in that room, but when they were out in the corridor and she had locked the door, she went on in her usual chiming voice: 'I'm so glad you like Adam. Mark and I are quite fond of him. It's so nice to be spied on by somebody who's so *like* one, don't you know.'

Downstairs Rose, who was now quite white, refused their offer of a lift.

'No, I'll take the tram. I would rather, really.'

Mark was pompously affectionate in his farewell. 'Rose, you simply must come and stay when you return Warsaw-wards. Alexandra and I insist.'

Adam was giving instructions to the driver of the hired car.

Thirty-one

At the stop outside the School of Engineering, Janet Rudowska pulled herself wearily on to the tram. While she stood among the crowd of people returning from work and waited to pay her fare, she noticed that Rose was sitting up in front. Rose's shoulders were hunched as though she huddled away from cold; she looked unprotected. Janet watched her with apprehension.

Apprehension — so often the feelings Janet had for her own family amounted only to this. Apprehension during the war, whenever she returned home on her leaves from the hospital. Apprehension growing as you approached Barnham up the asphalt drive and the school-building gave off a dull tone like a bell that someone has jarred against, a thrumming noise which was a mixture of banged radiators, shouting in corridors, wireless sets shrilling the Forces programme, and all the semi-articulate hums and moanings that are emitted by a mass of schoolboys. All that life beyond the green baize doors which had made her desperately shy as a child. Homecomings were always anguish. The greatest anguish had been when Nico was killed and there was nobody to protect her any more, but it was always there: every time she approached the green door of School House, her heart burst with being sorry for Daddy and hating Mummy.

Now when she saw Rose in front of her in the tram, she experienced that identical jab of hate. Their mother, aes-

thete and convert and flower-arranger, had always let it be
known that she had the finer perceptions; she had looked on
Janet, by then a staff nurse, as a plain member of an un-
privileged race, trying her best to be useful. And Rose was
the same, since her return from Krakow. Rose was special:
whatever happened to people, it happened to her differently.
Rose went off to meet her grand friends, and never said
where she was going.

Janet paid her fare and went and sat next to Rose. Rose
clutched her arm and gave her a half-blind look. 'I don't
want to talk.'

Once inside the flat, however, Rose talked and talked.

At the end she said: 'You won't tell Witek, will you?
Please.'

'No.'

The spoilt child was stopped in her tracks: their mother,
through Rose, had got her deserts at last. You could have
worked this all out from the beginning, at Barnham. But
because they were in Biala Gora, at the extreme edge of
the known world, everything was different. Family apprehensions could not exist in the presence of true fear.

Janet had known this fear since her arrival. She had
spoken the language badly and everyone took her for a
German. Only Witek could protect her then. The disasters
that followed, the confiscation of their savings, the police
terror, lack of food and the loss of their second child, were
a progression that was pointing in only one direction, towards their final destruction. The apprehensions of the
English middle class were a mockery compared to this, and
yet they had done their work. The Poles grew stockier,
squarer and uglier in those years, as though they were holding up the low sky with the brute strength of spines and
shoulders. Janet endured with her husband and with

friends like Krysia. But sometimes she felt that they had an idea of what happiness was, and she had not.

Even now, Rose was still demanding action.

'I'll keep him in England. I don't care what I promised Witek. I want to keep Tadeusz there for ever, away from this appalling place. I'll do anything you ask. He simply must not grow up here.'

'Let's not talk about it now, I want my tea.'

'I'll get it.' This was the first time Rose had offered to help with anything so simple.

Janet lay back on the divan, her eyes closed. Because with Rose you paid the full emotional cost of family life, she was more tired than ever.

Rose went into the kitchen. Tadeusz was standing by the table. There was no other door; he must have been there the whole time.

'Hullo,' he said.

Was he trembling at what he had overheard, or from the gaucheness, the minor stresses of adolescence? From now on she would never be able to tell what he was feeling. There were secrets everywhere and anybody could deceive Rose. Once you had heard of the existence of a world of lies, you felt their presence everywhere. Perhaps, under the influence of some drug or other, one might see a chair or a table as totally evil; it was a quality of perception like this.

Tadeusz slithered past her. He went into the sitting-room and began talking to his mother.

Beyond the door their voices rose and fell in the monotonous uncoloured English of exiles.

'Mrs. Kazimierska has telephoned. She wants to see Rose before she is leaving. She has a package for her to bring to England.'

'All right.'

'And about May Day Parade. I will be marching with my class but I can show Rose where to see best.'

His voice was raised, strained. Perhaps he was talking so that Rose would be able to overhear in the kitchen.

'Of course, darling,' Janet said. 'Why did you come back so early today?'

'It is because we must go back this evening for the meeting that is discussing our excursion.'

'Oh, I see.'

'I must go now, to fetch my colleagues.'

'Give me a kiss.'

When Tadeusz had left, Rose came in with two glasses of tea.

'Do you think he heard what we were saying?'

'What you were saying, Rose. I wasn't saying anything.'

Rose put down the tea. 'One tries to help, one does everything and —' she began to howl. 'Oh God, it's too awful here, awful. I want to go home.'

Thirty-two

O N the morning of the First of May Tadeusz led her into the middle of the town until they reached a spot on the pavement opposite the Party Headquarters. Exactly there, he left her. He had to join the contingent from his school, the Tenth Gymnasium, who were waiting in a side street nearly a mile away on the other side of the town.

Tadeusz ran through the streets against the crowd. Everything was closed for the holiday, but not many people were about for the Spring feast of the workers was a dying rite. No procession was taking place in the capital this year, and hardly anything even in Red Square, Moscow. Biala Gora kept the privilege because there had recently been disturbances in the factories and a pro-religious riot in a local industrial settlement. The procession here was a show of force.

When he arrived among his school-fellows, he took up his place without speaking to any of them. The sense of responsibility, which afflicted him very much at this time, made him feel dumb and rude. Even when he forgot Rose, he had the usual resentment at taking part in politically organized activity. He didn't want it to be either a success or a failure, yet he was annoyed when other people in his class made a joke of it. There was no point in being like them; you ended up half-sickened with boredom and frustration. He desperately wanted to do things properly, as his mother and Rose had told him they were done in England, but there seemed to be no chance.

After some preliminary shuffling and marking time, the contingent of the Tenth Gymnasium moved off. Now Tadeusz began to be irritated by Basia Wengorzewska, the girl marching in front of him. Couldn't she march straight, without wobbling and swaying around like that? A mass of hair, light brown but blonde-streaked as though it had been tumbled in fresh pollen, kept on escaping from underneath her cap. From time to time she glanced round her, and he tried to catch her eye to frown at her. But she was not watching, only seeing whether she was being watched. His agony grew. He longed to stop her and pull her together: she was so soft, so inadequate compared with the stolid girls marching on either side. He stared and stared at her until he felt dazed.

Meanwhile Rose felt she had been waiting for hours in front of the Party Headquarters. The local leaders were beginning to appear on the first floor balcony and above them the huge images of Marx, Gomulka and Lenin, bellying and shrinking in the fresh breeze, seemed alternately to smirk or to pull long faces at the crowd lining the street below. Rain earlier had wettened the party flags so that they had lost their brightness and were now the colour of an old nose-bleed. The wind has also twisted up the long streamers across the street. As a result they seldom showed more than one word at a time: Long Live . . . Peace . . . War . . . Capitalism . . . Reconstruction. Twigs were being blown off the trees and Rose felt one of them falling past her face. She picked it up. The plane trees blossoms were just unfolding on it, yellow-green, with the flower stalks still as fragile as stamens. She held it up and yawned, and let the unborn flowers flick against her cheek.

Now, from the inner recesses of the plane trees, loud-speakers crackled into full voice. The march past began, stopped for a speech, for applause and for ritual shouting, and began again. How small the factory-workers were, particularly the older ones! They wore berets or cloth caps, raincoats or blue-grey jerseys with zip-fronts. Their faces were grey and expressionless. Because of the recent disturbances participation was compulsory and their sections took an age to go past. With the exception of a few medalled veterans on Armistice Days, Rose had never seen civilians march like this and it felt wrong. This should have been a march of protest. They should be protesting now, because they were so poor, so ill-dressed, so ugly with their swinging work-distorted heads. Yet as they passed the balcony and the huge floating faces (Lenin, blown to one side now, was showing his back to the other two) each man stiffened, straightened his arms and turned eyes right.

After half an hour, the sheer weight of numbers began to make its effect. Every public demonstration, if it is massive enough, creates this willing doubt. It becomes the reality itself. Individual protest is eccentricity; private reservations are merely reflex twitches like those a dog makes when it is dreaming. The tramp of boots on the cobbles, the applauding spectators, the desperately cheerful music blot out everything. Long live the First of May!

Long live the First of May! The slogan is meaningless, but what does anybody's protest mean? If you are Adam, nothing at all. For him all arguments end in nihilism. He is still in the Labour Camps, less free than any of these workers. He is out of date but not far enough. To protest now you need to remember far back to a time, infinitely long ago to Rose, when she was a small child. Then you can remember what it was to be free. And who can remember,

except for the old has-beens, people like Krystyna Kazimierska? At least you would never find her taking part in this
drilled stampede past Party Headquarters.

By now Rose was completely involved, her throat sore
and her eyes smarting with tears. She couldn't decide what
she thought about the onset of the school children, who
seemed to bring a lightening of the atmosphere, a flicker of
smiles along the stolid length of spectators on the opposite
side of the street. Brought up at a school, she was used to
smiling at the seriousness children bring to a rigmarole of
no real importance; it was hard to do that here with old
Karl Marx flapping away like a luffing mainsail against the
building over there. All she could do was feel a pang of
sympathy for the plain faces of the little girls above the
nineteenth-century uniforms with sailor collars, and feel
pleased, too, that nobody had wasted time on teaching them
to march properly. And a moment later all this was forgotten in the tenseness of knowing that Tadeusz was
approaching, of feeling his presence like a wave washing
along between these two banks of onlookers.

His class was the best turned out, except for Basia Wengorzewska, pink-faced with exertion now, pouting with
boredom and always out of step: an infant Bardot whose
sulks made everyone's seriousness seem doltish. But Rose
did not notice her at all. Her eyes were on Tadeusz.

Thirty-three

H E, however, had completely forgotten about her. Once, at an intersection of streets near the Main Post Office, he failed to see that the line in front was marking time; he stumbled straight into Basia, collided on to the soft shock of her warmth and retreated, slightly overwhelmed. Trying to think of something different, he looked at the clock on the Post Office. It was after eleven, past the time when he usually had his 'second breakfast' but he didn't feel hungry. The line stopped there for about ten minutes and then they moved off again. Basia kept tripping over the cobbles where they had risen up under the winter's frosts.

At about ten yards from the balcony, he glanced up. Rose wasn't waving or anything else, just staring at him, and for the first time for several days they looked each other in the face.

Then he blushed, until his face grew quite shiny. He laughed; the laugh fluttered and trembled all over his face. The moment was a long one and in its confusion he forgot to turn to the balcony, to the row of dark suits, and the steel-rimmed spectacles which were just beginning to glint in the first sunshine of that day.

Then he was gone.

Rose was ridiculously gratified. At first she could not tell why, except that Tadeusz had not looked at the row of

Party bigwigs but at her instead. Then she knew it was because she had got through to him at last.

The sun was really shining now and all round people were smiling and nudging each other into attention.

From a window one floor above the balcony and invisible to its load of occupants, a small man had set out to grapple with the recalcitrant image of Lenin. There was a rope round his waist and the heavy brown façade of the nineteenth-century German building afforded him plenty of holds. Above him the great banner, free of its guy ropes, swooped backwards and forwards on the wind. His hand flew out, like a white star on the dark brickwork, seized one of the flying ropes and hauled it in. Mouths were open in the crowd and nobody spoke. The march past of children continued but now only the most devoted parents were watching it. With the finicky attentiveness of an ant selecting and trundling a fragment of twig, the man tied the rope tightly down on to the front of the building. At length he looked down, expecting some silent evidence of praise from the face upturned beneath him. Above, the banner hung motionless. From where he was, he could not see that it was the wrong way out: beside Marx and Gomulka hung a blank sheet, where Vladimir Ilyich had finally turned his face to the wall.

The crowd enjoyed this very quietly. But, as the last contingents of children gave way to the first deputations from the University, militiamen began signalling to the little man on the windowsill. The officials on the balcony, disquieted by all the attention they had seemed to be receiving, began squinnying upwards into the sunlight. Even the professors and students broke step to watch what was going on. One of their number, however, was determined to pretend that nothing odd was happening. At exactly the correct moment Witek's head turned rigidly towards the building and then forward again. Witek did not see Rose at all.

A minute later, in the contingent from the Faculty of History, Rose saw the tall striding figure of Krysia Kazimierska, and this seemed the final evidence of fear, of the naked power still generated by the drab group on the balcony.

As soon as the parade was finished, the onlookers flooded out over the streets and began hurrying home. Tadeusz made his way back against the crowd to fetch Rose but, when he reached the place where she had stood all morning, he found her gone.

Rose walked to the tram stop and then took fright at the rush of shoving, short-tempered people. She remembered that Tadeusz had promised to come back for her but now it was too late to look for him. Frustrated, she decided to wait until the trams were emptier, and to sit down for a while and think.

But as people do who intend to go away and think, she soon gave herself up to exorbitant fantasy. From this morning she had already made up her mind that, while other people including Adam were venal time-servers, Witek actually enjoyed the world he inhabited. That it was ultimately terrifying she knew from seeing Mrs. Kazimierska marching by. And above all she believed that Tadeusz's blushes meant that now he was properly humiliated by it, and must be rescued, which was what she was going to do. These thoughts took perhaps the minute or two in which she was looking for a seat on one of the park benches. Once she sat down she was off dreaming about having Tadeusz in London with her. Having Tadeusz was a compensation for the loss of Adam.

An hour later she arrived home. She let herself quietly

into the hallway, because there was nearly always work in progress somewhere in the flat. Now, though, there was the sound of violent quarrelling, breathing silence, then sobbing. She stood for a moment wondering what to do.

Then she decided to go in. It would give Witek and Janet a rest: they usually desisted in her presence. She opened the door.

Janet had her back turned. Witek was sitting on one of the divans: it was he who was weeping.

He saw Rose first, and rushed at her. 'There she is!'

Thirty-four

A T first everything was confusion and shouting.

Rose sat down. 'Please, please tell me what has happened.'

Witek was in full cry and could not easily be brought back to the beginning. 'She says, Tell me what's happened! ' He stood over her. '*You* tell *me* nothing at all. Why did you come here? I think you came here to Poland because of love. I forget that you English do not love your families at all. Yes, I can tell that the minute I meet your family at Barnham. It is all cold and unhappy. You do not love each other at all.'

For a time the sisters were too scorched by this to speak.

'You English go away to find — to found colonies because you do not love each other at all.'

Rose was frightened now. As soon as there was no possibility of thinking him ridiculous, all her English resources would be gone. 'Please, please, what has happened?'

'The money. Why didn't you tell about the money?'

'Oh. That.'

'Yes. Speak, please.'

'We — we thought it might make things difficult for you.' Rose was determined not to be alone in this. 'Janet knew, too.'

'She is always against me now,' said Witek quietly. 'But you, Rose, can you tell the truth?'

'That is true. And because of your beliefs.'

'My beliefs! *Boze*, you think I am a child?'

'I wanted to be helpful, really I did.'

'So you did not tell me about this money. Because you wanted to be helpful. Because of my beliefs. Yet why are you telling everyone else?'

'That's not true. And I won't be shouted at. I never told a soul, did I, Janet?'

'I don't know, Rose. Didn't you?'

'Oh, blast you, you might at least help. Can I have a cigarette?'

Witek pushed the box towards her. 'You told this Dr. Karpinski who you know wants my job.'

'No, that's not true, Witek.'

'It is true, you went off to Zakopane with him?' The place name for him had a sexual weight: something like Brighton or Atlantic City. 'It is true?'

Rose was silent. She twitched her shoulders and said: 'Very well. Yes.'

'Then you told him. You knew who he was and what he was trying to do to me, to my career. You and he . . .' His voice ran into a dry patch. He seemed ready to weep again. 'You told him.'

'I didn't. It may sound silly when I explain it. But here in Poland there is something competitive about misfortune. When we come from the West we don't want to say how well off we are. You make us feel ashamed, as though we had cheated to get what we have. So I didn't tell Adam. In fact, if you want to know another silly thing, I told him Daddy had been a master at a grammar school, not a public school.'

Witek was not much interested in these subtleties.

'Whether you tell him or not, he knew. Perhaps he was reading your letters.'

'I didn't have anything written down. I was advised not to —' She broke off. When she remembered who had given her this advice, everything was quite clear.

'It makes no difference, Rose. Whatever happened, he informs the Party and they accuse me that I have large reserves of foreign currency which I have not declared. Not only my future job is in danger but also my present one. In fact, we are all in danger.'

'Oh, Witek darling, how awful.'

'Darling, now. And you still deny it?'

'Yes, I do. You must stop bullying me. I know I was wrong about Adam Karpinski but so was everybody else. I didn't believe anybody could be like that. I happen not to be used to lies.'

He pounced on this last phrase.

'Not used to lies! She says, not used to lies! Rose, you have been lying since you first set your foot through that door.'

At this point she broke into tears.

He watched her closely. He was extremely conscious of the erotic aspects of distress. When she bowed her head, with the fine hair scented by the fragrant shampoos she brought from England and her face damp and agonized, she was at least half-raped in his mind. He ached with unused violence because he could not hit a woman he had never slept with. Trembling, he recovered himself.

Janet patted him on the shoulder. 'Better leave her, old boy.' There was more understanding in her voice than was quite decent. The thing resembled those moments of extreme intimacy when all behaviour is imperiously dictated.

The sisters were alone.

'Here's some tea.'

'I don't want any, thank you.'

'Cheer up. Things like this have happened before and we have always managed to pick up the pieces.'

'You sound like the W.V.S.,' Rose said.

'What?'

'Nothing.' Rose blew her nose and wiped her eyes. 'Actually, I know now exactly what happened. It was that frightful bitch who told Adam. She probably thought it was fearfully amusing.'

'Who?'

'Alexandra Tatham. You see, old Mark has always been a bit of a *coureur* and when she saw that I —'

'Oh God. Here we go again.'

'What?'

'Nothing. Nothing, Rose.'

Rose kept an offended silence while Janet drank her tea.

'Witek and I'll get over this, never you fear. In the old days it was dangerous to admit you had relatives abroad. You remember those desperately cheerful letters I used to write? Now, it'll be all right. It isn't as if we had ever seen any of the money. Witek will be able to explain it all away, he is very good at that sort of thing and he has the right friends.'

Rose was doubtful. She was the only one who knew Adam personally. Whatever they might think of him, he had twice the brains and force of Witek, and he would not be easy to choke off. To Rose the path was still wide open to disaster.

'Witek doesn't know about our plans for Tadeusz?'

'No. But that's done with now, isn't it?'

'I suppose so,' Rose said. 'What's going to happen to you?'

'You might have asked that a bit sooner, I must say. All I want is some peace. It will be better when you have gone.'

'Yes,' said Rose. 'It will.'

When Tadeusz came in, Rose questioned him about the May Day Parade. It was her last chance to make him feel with her. 'You didn't seem to be enjoying it very much, if I may say so.'

Tadeusz blushed. 'I was.'

'Were you? Sorry.'

'I was enjoying it very much,' he said sullenly. 'I was proud to be with my school-mates.'

Rose sighed with disappointment. Even that compensation was to be taken away. But perhaps Tadeusz's social activities were a phase parallel to that of the boys at Barnham, who would lose all charm and grow sourly humourless just before Confirmation. It was the sore, creaking stage in the evolution of the dragonfly.

Thirty-five

A FEW days later he departed at three in the morning on his excursion to the mountains. Breathing like a pack-animal under his apparatus of canvas and rubber, he clumped through the room in which Rose was lying awake, and went out into the asphalt silence before sunrise, when pigeons and motor-cycles were still locked away, and a taxi was depositing the last drunks outside the doors of the apartment buildings.

Rose spent most of the day typing out translations for the Rudowskis. There were times when she imagined she would go to Warsaw to look for Adam. But she knew she would not because, like Janet, she was tired. She was glad to have a firm booking on the LOT plane to London, leaving in five days' time.

In the late afternoon she went into town to visit Mrs. Kazimierska.

'Come in, Rose. My husband is at a hospital conference, so you will not meet him after all. In any case he is not very interesting.'

The flat, which Rose was visiting for the the first time, was half-dark, crammed with furniture and heavy with the smell of furniture polish and cabbage.

'These things were all mother's. You see, our own house was in Warsaw. When we returned after the Rising — look, I will show you what we found.' She rummaged in a drawer and brought out half a blue and gold china plate. 'I found that in what used to be our garden. Our son and daughter were both killed, you know, so this is all we have from before the war.'

Rose looked stiff and slightly offended.

Mrs. Kazimierska laughed suddenly. She put back the plate and slammed the drawer. 'And how has it been, dear Rose.'

'Terrible.'

'That I can easily believe. Mr. Rudowski is a difficult proposition.'

'It is my fault, too. It seems none of us can say anything we mean. When I was a child we had a nanny like that. She was so easily shocked that in the end everybody told her lies.'

Mrs. Kazimierska looked at her with some detachment.

'*We* had an English nanny,' she said, 'and everybody confessed everything to her, even my dear brothers. The water is now boiling. Nescafé?'

She mixed in the sharp-smelling powder and poured out two cups.

'It is because Rudowski is so stupid,' she said. 'Intelligent people can always converse, whatever their politics.'

'I'm afraid it isn't just him. When I first saw Janet again and realized properly all she had suffered, I thought I couldn't do enough for her. But in fact it made me hate her. Not just because we are sisters, I mean — she was always quite nice to me when I was small. It's because of everything here.'

'I think I understand. When relatives sometimes send me a parcel, I can hardly bring myself to thank them for it.'

'Has this happened to everyone?'

'When our friends come from abroad it is often like

that. It is so impossible to explain things, we give up trying. When I told you just now about the Warsaw Rising, you were very, very bored.'

'Oh, I am sorry, I didn't mean —'

'Young people here are the same. It is sad but it is true. All the same, I am sure you are glad you have been here.'

'No. I'm afraid I wish I'd never come, if it meant finding them both so miserable.'

'You must know enough about the Rudowskis now, but perhaps they are not so miserable as you think. One thing perhaps I can tell you: she will never leave him.'

'I know she won't,' Rose said. 'Isn't it awful?'

On her way home, carrying the parcel for Mrs. Kazimierska's niece, she went into the Self-Service, looking for something to take back with her. Beyond the bare necessities the only things on sale were greyish packets of soup mix and the glass jars of Bulgarian apricots which, when you attempted to open them, left your hands covered with blood. Instead she bought a bottle of Georgian wine.

Janet was still out. Rose opened the bottle of wine, sweetish, tasting slightly of prunes. She searched in Janet's shelves for something to read. She pulled out an anthology of modern verse and leafed right through it, finding nothing to attract her attention beyond the first few lines, until she got to Yeats:

> That girls at puberty should find
> Original Adam in their thought —

She banged the book shut, put it quickly back in the shelf, even adjusting the other books so that no one could see it had been taken out. Then she heard the clink of the bicycles in the passage and knew Witek was coming through the flat towards her.

Thirty-six

H E stood in the doorway, visibly making up his mind whether or not he was about to step into the middle of a baited trap. When he saw her lying on the divan, quick and tricky as she was, the project became worthwhile.

'Witek, have some wine,' she said sharply.

The effort at welcome in her voice did not work out as she meant it to, but he was too intent to notice. Chuckling at something — perhaps it was the fact that she had been out, had actually bought the wine and then opened it all by herself — he sat down at the table. He picked up the bottle and examined the label closely.

'Please translate what it says.'

'"Sweet Table Wine". Is that correct?'

'Damn, I thought it must be. Anyway, have some. I'll get a glass.'

He looked appreciatively at the glass and laughed again. Then formality descended on him: he had already decided on no account to be put off. Pulling a small memorandum out of his pocket, he proceeded to install his own special type of social unease.

'I —' they both said at once.

'No, please.'

'No, you go on, Witek. I had nothing important to say,' she shrugged. 'How could I?'

'Very well, I have one or two points that I wish to discuss.'

She put her feet up again, getting more comfortable. 'Go ahead.'

He gave her legs a haggard look.

'I was wondering if before you leave us you will be willing to record your voice for our department? It would be most helpful to us in our work. Janet has not the time, also it seems to me her voice acquired some Polish intonations which cause it to be less good for us.'

'All right. Tell me when.'

'Monday morning, then? Now to my second point.'

He was silent for a while and she watched him labouring at it.

'With regard to this second point we must be very careful. It is about this money.'

Another silence.

'I think, I think'—he coiled a little with embarrassment—'that you were discreet, and that Dr. Karpinski found out through other sources.'

'Well, thank you!'

He laughed miserably. 'In fact you were so discreet that I was not informed! However, you have appreciated that the situation is difficult for me to understand. You see, here the salaries are—well, in higher education they are —well, most people have no money at all. Also it seems to me, if this money comes to Tadeusz, it must by law be transferred into our currency.'

'I know that, Witek.'

'You have observed our position. It is not easy. With a car, for instance, you see—'

'But it all belongs to Tadeusz.'

'A car.' He sipped some wine. 'That would make all the difference.'

He was much out of his depth about the money and could be fuddled by an appeal to English legality, which is universally considered respectable.

'We have laws, too, Witek. I don't even know if the money can leave England. In any case you keep saying it will damage your position with your job.'

'That is my third point.' He gently hiccuped. 'Today I have a long and very valuable talk with Dr. Zwiersz. I think you don't know him, he is the chief representative of our Party at the University. Naturally I was explaining to him how this rumour about the money is false. And he in return told me that it is very uncertain that Karpinski comes here. He is unwilling to give up all his jobs in Warsaw. Dr. Zwiersz insists he must, for the students' sake. Dr. Zwiersz is very good to the students.'

'So, after all this bloodiness, there is no danger for you at all?'

'There is always danger when nothing is certain. I have many problems still. There is Janet, she is very unsettled. And Tadeusz. You wanted him to visit England, he is impressionable and not sure of himself. That is the fourth point I had for discussion.'

'I thought as much. I have no rights now, have I?'

'After all this trouble of course he must stay here. With this money of his you might keep him in England.'

'What a beastly thing to say!'

He shook his head. 'Rose, you have shown you do not understand some problems here.'

She ran her hands through her hair. 'Oh, what's the use? You meet nobody, you and Janet. The other Poles aren't like you: they — they have free souls.'

He looked nasty at this, 'I think you did not know those people so well. You could be disappointed.'

'All right. All right.'

Witek sat back and finished his wine.

He had won. At every moment his score was going up. His future expanded and soared like a balloon hard with gas. In a short time he would have a permanent place in the academic world, and earn a respect that he would never have known as a language teacher. He would be able to tap that reservoir of deference that still existed years after the death of an artistocratic society, he would be called 'Professor' by concierges and sellers of cabbage. His promotion would help Tadeusz as well, for university examiners were benevolent to the children of academic colleagues.

And in addition there now might be the bonus of a car, perhaps ever a summer cottage in the mountains.

At the same time he knew that when Rose left he was going to be as miserable and unsettled as Janet was. On all counts Rose had bequeathed nothing but disquiet. Witek had always thought he agreed with arguments against the West; in his wartime memories, England had looked very like Biala Gora today. But he was the child of Silesian farmers, and materialism was a terrible temptation to him. He hated to be ascetic: let others play chess and listen to Szymanowski! He wanted to feel things solid in his hands, the good finish, the safe shininess that would not wear away. He thought of Rose's stockings, the neatness of her pants and suspender belt lying round the flat. He would have pretty students from time to time but he would never again get in range of anyone like this girl who was sitting in front of him, her complexion dulled

a little by tiredness, but her hair bright and her body small
and firm.

'Rose,' he said very quietly.

'Yes?'

'Rose, please let us part as good friends. It is important
to me.'

'You've won, Witek. Isn't that enough?'

'No, it is not.'

'Please, Witek. No!'

She stood up and pushed the round table at him, so that
the edge caught him in the stomach. Then they were both
quiet, hearing Janet come in.

Thirty-seven

THE telephone rang while they were at supper on Sunday evening.

Janet spoke briefly and handed the receiver to Witek.

'*Tu Rudowski.*'

With his tongue exploring his teeth for a fragment of sausage skin he listened.

'*Tak.*'

His mouth was still, and his face gradually set rigid.

'*Tak.*'

From across the room the women could hear an urgent voice rising and falling on a flood of narrative. Witek did not move.

'*Tak, tak.*'

Rose looked enquiringly at her sister. So far Witek had said nothing more than 'Yes', but Janet's head was bowed towards the table and her fists were clenching and unclenching.

'Janet!' Witek called to her and she stared fixedly at him. Now he began to speak, with his face still grim and his eyes held by hers. The words buzzed, repeated and insisted until, after about four minutes, he put the telephone down and there was silence. Witek was gazing straight at Rose and she put on an enquiring expression to attract his attention, but he was not seeing her at all. Still in silence he dialled a number, then spoke again.

Janet gave Rose a small indifferent smile.

' Is it something about Tadeusz? '

' Yes.'

' Serious? '

' We don't know yet. He's had a fall. He's got concussion and they've taken him to hospital. Witek's putting a call through to the hospital now.'

Rose made lines with a fork on the tablecloth. Would they accuse her of communicating a disease of clumsiness which causes people to fall off mountains?

When Witek at length came back to the supper table, his normal manner, of heavy politeness, had quite gone. He looked solid and blunt and might never have had an ambition in his life. Still, out of civility to Rose, he spoke in English.

' I have a colleague who has a motor-cycle. I think he will drive me there tonight.'

' Is it very bad? ' Rose asked.

The Rudowskis turned to her as though this curiosity from a bystander occasioned them some surprise. Rose felt herself slipping out of their lives at last.

' It's concussion and his leg is perhaps broken. Nothing else.'

' Thank God.' But they made Rose feel it was not her business to say this.

While Witek telephoned his colleague, Rose began putting the supper things together. Obviously they were not going to be eating any more. She was herself afflicted by nervous pangs of hunger and, once through the kitchen door, she quickly devoured some slices of sausage and licked her fingers. Tadeusz's bed, flat and empty with the blankets folded up, accused her of callousness but she was unconvinced. Did she feel so detached because she was seldom

quite sure what was going on? Or because Tadeusz falling
off a mountain came too late in a long progression of
shocks and portents and disequilibria?

Outside in the twilight they found Witek's colleague:
another small and solid man.

After handshakes and farewells, the motor-cycle roared
and spluttered off towards the main road. There was a hint
of wartime in this bleak departure, and in the image of
the two men on the little machine pitting themselves
against all that distance. It was also a very Polish image:
only human beings, loved or hated, could give meaning
to the bare landscape and the looming approach of night.

Janet took Rose's arm. 'I do hope he'll be all right.'

'I'm sure the hospital is looking after him.'

'No, I mean Witek.'

'What could go wrong with him?'

'Oh, it's dark, and a long way, and at night it's dangerous, there are drunk peasants lurching all over the
roads.' They walked slowly back to the door of the building.
'If only we had a car! God, why is life so hard? Why?'

Rose, who for the first time wanted to cry, squeezed
her arm. 'Let's do some work. I'm sure it's the only
thing.'

Janet dictated translations of two articles on plant disease
and her sister took them down in shorthand. They spent
a good deal of time leafing through a technical dictionary
whose accuracy they did not trust, and checking it with
the Shorter Oxford. When Rose had typed out the articles
there were so many further corrections to be made that she
had to do them again. They were working to fill in time
and yet, despite a nagging anxiety, felt comfortable and
easy together in a way they had not experienced till now.
It was nearly midnight when they finished. Both were ex-

hausted. The telephone rang while Rose was in the kitchen making tea. When Janet had replaced the receiver she came through to the kitchen.

'Tadeusz is all right. He's quite conscious and talking. Poor old Witek sounds in a terrible state though. He's starting back now as he has early classes tomorrow. I suppose he'll get here some time in the small hours.'

Rose, who was sitting up in bed with her face still starched with sleep, was trying to discover what was going on. It was half past five in the morning. Witek was shouting. It was a noise that had been going on for some time, but she had woken into the middle of it.

Perhaps this time he had become insane.

For Rose's sake, he tried to curse in English, but contact with Janet had provided him with no word much stronger than 'beastly'. He went back to Polish. There too words failed him; he knew no distinction between sincerity and violence. When you really meant anything, you broke things. He now destroyed two folk art vases and tore up a square of peasant weave. They did not much matter, but Rose was shocked and frightened; she had the wincing, English respect for property.

In retreat, she put her head under the pillow and stayed there, glad that Witek had no sense of the ridiculous and hoping that, when she returned to the light, everything would somehow have changed.

Janet had disappeared, Witek sat at the table, weeping. He was still in his plastic raincoat, and the dust of the country roads shadowed his eye-sockets and ran down in dark trickles with his tears. He stared out on to a prospect of misery, a man endlessly betrayed by his women.

Rose emerged from under her pillow, dishevelled, with

hair all over a hot face, and asked: 'What am I supposed
to have done now?'

'You tried to steal my son from me, that is all. He heard
you tell Janet about it. All the time you plan to deceive
me, from the very beginning. You make him fond of you
so that he is frightened to tell me. He tried to kill himself
in the mountains because he could not think of any way
to get away from you. He walked and walked and hoped
he would die. But they were finding him in time.'

'No.'

'This is true and all the other things too.'

It was no use telling him that the plans had been Janet's;
after all, she had not told Janet of Witek's blundering
passes at her. Peace must come now, with the causes of
war undecided, with everything important unsaid. Meanwhile she listened to Witek's wild cry, the cry of a man
always excluded from the possibilities of life.

'Why did you work against me, Rose? Why am I always
so disgusting and dismissed and dishonourable? I am doing
the best for my son. Rose, this is a terrible world we are
in here, and you come — you come from Kensington and
you try to ruin everything.' He stopped. In a silence he
said: 'You ruin my poor life.'

And so she had it at last, if she wanted it: the stiletto
thrust of her victory — his admission that he hated his
life. It was what she had shamelessly worked for, and it
was now quite useless to her. The end was here, now. She
did not speak.

Janet came out of the kitchen. Rose watched her with
a sudden imploring sympathy.

'Don't worry about me,' Janet said briskly. 'I shall be
all right. Just leave here as soon as possible. That's all
I want now.'

Thirty-eight

To and fro the train rattled on ill-found sleepers. Alternately Rose felt the upholstered right haunch of the woman on her left, the upholstered left haunch of the man on her right. First they had gazed at her luggage with suspicion, then settled down into fat silence, members of a potato-eating race well adapted to the unending discomfort of train journeys.

The train was slowly proceeding through a marshy landscape near the remains of a prehistoric lake village. From time to time its whistle gave out a ringing, lacustrine cry, the sort of cry that wild fauna might have emitted across these Tennysonian meres on every rainy afternoon since the Ice Age. Rain spat again and again on the windows. Today was one of the chill weeping days in the early part of May, the days of the Ice Saints, St. Pancras, St. Servace and St. Boniface, whose arrival affords a reminder that all is by no means well with the year. If you had confidence in the Spring, your trust was misplaced: it will let you down. And if you are a pessimist you can give the satisfied snort of those whose worst fears are justified, and continue toting the burden of existence a little further on.

For Rose, who looked forward to nothing at all, the day remained abysmally sad. She was returning to London. God must come and blast the inhabitants of Beauchamp Place, and frizzle up those on the pavements outside

Harrods. Only then, surely, could He bring about a balance of the world's pain.

The carriage was darkened by someone standing in the doorway.

'Please, you remember me?'

At the first words of a foreign language the faces of the other passengers stiffened: they were no longer present. To Rose the questions sounded oddly humble. Here was someone who knew her yet did not know how far down the hill she had actually gone. He was a tall young man wearing a beret, and a black sweater which was hidden under another of those smelly plastic raincoats.

'Of course I remember you!' But the puzzle in her voice told him clearly that she had forgotten his name.

'Miroslaw Sypniewski.'

'Mirek, of course.'

She surprised him by getting to her feet at once. Half-stumbling across her neighbour's plump legs, she arrived beside Mirek in the corridor, like a swimmer grabbing the boat's edge.

'You remember the evening at the Students' Club?'

'Of course I remember. You were very sad.'

He laughed. 'Where are you travelling now?'

'To Warsaw.'

'You are staying with friends?'

'No, I'm going home.'

And so he looked sad again. 'I think you are pleased,' he said though her voice had given him no cause to think this.

'No, I'm not. Everything has gone wrong, you see, and I had hoped for so much.'

'In this country we must be very careful with hope.'

'I know.'

A station drew up outside the window. Loud speakers were playing elderly cheerful music but inside the train it was quiet.

'What happened to Derek?' Rose asked suddenly.

'He has left. But his girl has not yet got the English visa. She is awaiting in Biala Gora. I think there is some difficulty.'

'There might easily be. What's she like really?'

He shrugged. 'She is the first Polish girl Derek is getting to know. For him perhaps it is different. But it is a pity, I think.'

She liked him for his sympathy. He was a really kind man. Of course Loasby had distrusted him, but even now, after everything else that had happened to her, she was certain that Loasby was wrong. She watched Mirek's tall body swaying to and fro in front of her and felt a curious sensation of peace. He had been appointed to lead her out of this wilderness and into the sane world.

'I can understand about Derek. One feels, if one had started with different people, everything would have turned out differently. One might have discovered something.'

Mirek looked at her ruminatively. 'I'm afraid you don't have a very good impression.'

'I do, really.'

'Not really, I'm afraid.' He laughed. 'When is your aeroplane?'

'This afternoon. At four o'clock. The LOT plane.'

'I may take you to the airport?'

'Oh, please do.'

The train started again. As they approached the Warsaw area, the sandy earth along the track began breaking out with the spiked vegetation of the seashore. Though Poland is in the heart of Europe, much of it looks as though it

were near the edge of the sea. Rose and Mirek stood talking in the corridor; in his presence there was never any
sense of strain. He bought her a scorching glass of tea.
When the ticket collector came round, he was obliged to
pay extra.

'Why do they make you do that? I thought you were
a student and paid half fare anyway.'

'It is nothing. It is not important.' He seemed embarrassed.

Later she saw that he had been given a new ticket. She
realized then that he had intended getting off at the last
station. Now, for her sake, he was coming on to Warsaw,
even though, after today, he would not be seeing her again.
Because he had been in prison, he could never leave Poland.
His kindness was like a small bunch of roses at the end of
an arduous journey.

Two hours later they were in the airport shed.

Around them stood the strangely clad members of an
excursion of American Poles, escorted by their own priest.
All of them had the shiny coarseness given by a generation
or two in the Middle West, but under this they kept a
look of their forebears, of people like Witek, for instance,
or of the passengers in the train. None of them looked at
all like Mirek. He and Rose stood apart, without talking.
A whole cloud of possible emotions made them distrust
speech.

The tourists spoke a mixture of Polish and American.
Now and then while they talked, they slapped at their
chests and sides as though stabbed by pain. There the hand
felt the limp oblong and was reassured. Then a doubt;
might it after all be only a forgotten wallet or a neglected
letter? And so they fished out the olive-green passport and

stared at it for a moment, as intently as in a mirror; it was their reality. Their faces lost anxiety and they looked as though they had just been kissed.

The sight of these people, the strident result of so much that is both desired and detested, had finally driven Rose and Mirek speechless; there was so little to say and so much to explain. At last a stewardess shepherded the excursion through into the customs. Rose kissed Mirek quickly, and followed.

By the gate on to the airfield there was almost a stampede: elbows thrusting, feet stamping, silence and laboured breath, as the visitors fought once more to escape from the soil of their ancestors.

Again Rose stayed till last.

Looking back, she saw Mirek standing in his pale raincoat behind a wire fence, and beyond him a whole landscape waiting for explanation.

THE END